SCORPION TRAP

Soul Eater #4

PIPPA DACOSTA

'Scorpion Trap'

#4 Soul Eater

Pippa DaCosta

Urban Fantasy & Science Fiction Author

Subscribe to her mailing list here & get free ebooks.

Edited for US readers in US English.

Version 1.

Print ISBN-13: 978-1548059408

Print ISBN-10: 1548059404

www.pippadacosta.com

SUMMARY

"Given a choice, I'd prefer never to return to Egypt. Isis doesn't do choices."

The old world is dead. Legend tells us the gods are myths. But some remain, like a noose around Ace Dante's neck. And none are more dangerous than Isis. She demands the Soul Eater return to the land time forgot, break into a newly discovered tomb, and retrieve the skull from the sarcophagus inside. If Ace does this one thing, Isis will reveal the secrets he desperately seeks.

Ace knows there's a catch, there always is, but the truth is far worse than even he can imagine.

As Isis's true intentions unravel, so does Ace's past, leaving him no choice at all.

History is wrong.

The past is a lie.

And for the Soul Eater, the truth found in Egypt is far more terrifying than any god.

CHAPTER 1

The McDonald's tucked away behind the lingerie in Macy's was the last place I'd expected Shu to frequent, but there she was, carving through the unsuspecting crowd, her distinctive oil-black hair pulled into a scorpion-like ponytail, her stilettos stabbing into the sticky floor. She looked like the type of woman who would walk over cold corpses each morning to get her chai tea latte fix.

It wasn't that I didn't trust her. Lately, we'd been getting along fine, or as fine as a demon sorceress and soul eater could. That was the problem. In five hundred years, give or take a few decades, we'd never gotten along. She hated me. I hated her. Enemies cursed together for eternity. That made sense. What didn't make sense was her giving up a chance at redemption. Hell, had we been BFFs, she should have damn well taken Anubis's offer. She hadn't, and that was why I'd been tailing her for the past couple of weeks.

I sauntered into the line of folks waiting to collect their bagged orders and pretended to check my phone while keeping Shu in the corner of my eye. She'd stopped at a table by the window. Four twenty-somethings, two guys and two girls, abruptly quit chatting over hamburgers and looked up. Shu addressed them with a jerk of her chin. Tension crackled off her rapt crowd. I wondered if a brawl might be about to kick off when one of them wordlessly dusted off his hands and scooped a bag off the floor.

A family of five blocked my line of sight, forcing me to ditch the line and skirt the crowd for a better view. By the time I took up a spot near a stack of trays, Shu and the guy were exchanging packages. Cash would land in Shu's hands, and in his hands, I'd likely find a minor talisman or a small handwritten scroll and a bottle of sand, for effect. These four, in their pencil skirts and pressed shirts, would be in the market for career-boosting spells. Harmless, just like the spells for the last two buyers I shook down.

The deal concluded, and Shu left the young professionals and strode toward the exit. All four in the group watched her go until she'd almost slipped back into Macy's lingerie. I pushed away from the wall and was about to resume my stalking, when the buyer picked up a McDonald's napkin, hastily scrawled something on the paper, and with a flick of his fingers, lit it on fire. The napkin vanished in a blink—turned to ash. None of the diners noticed. Nobody but me.

I eased back against the tray rack. That little flourish of magic had just earned Shu's buyer a place on my watch list. Another sorcerer? Maybe Shu hadn't sold him a harmless spell after all.

The four professionals packed away their phones, shrugged on their jackets, and hitched up their bags, back to smiles and small talk. I trailed them through the lingerie displays and stuck with the buyer when they each split up without a goodbye between them. He sauntered through the kitchenware aisle, his swagger down to an art, and boarded the escalator heading down. A few shoppers behind, I leaned on the rail and got a good look between the spine of escalators that made up Macy's middle and fed shoppers in and out of ten floors of all-you-can-buy retail.

Mr. Swagger hit Floor 6, sprang from the escalator like a horse from its stall, veered back on himself, and shoved his way down the adjacent escalator. He stopped long enough to glance up, right at me, and toss me a salute. Then he was off again, shoving shoppers out of his path like bowling pins.

Why do they always have to run?

All pretense of stealth gone, I shoved past angsty shoppers, ignoring their bleats of alarm, and bolted after the cocky bastard. Some days, it would be so much easier to be the monster who stripped souls from bodies like peas from their pods. You'd be surprised how much easier it is to get around when you're made of sand and smoke. Couldn't do that in Macy's, though. Wasn't worth the godly fallout.

The cocky bastard had a decent head start, but I had the benefit of carving through his wake of surprised civilians. I was on him in seconds, my grip locked on the lapels of his expensive jacket so I could hang him up against a wall beside a stack of folded Levis and expressionless mannequins.

"Whoa, buddy," he stammered. "Whoa, whoa—Okay, okay, easy—"

"What were the hand theatrics back there?" I demanded.

"Hey, you're out of line." Cocky Bastard raised his voice, and despite having my face in his, he wasn't nearly as afraid as he should have been.

Shoppers stopped and gawked. Someone pulled a phone from their pocket. I didn't have the sword or coat on me, but that didn't mean I wanted my face all over the internet. Store security wouldn't be far behind either.

I dropped the cocky bastard onto his feet and squeezed his shoulder. "Ah, c'mon, Steve. I was just screwing with you, man."

He grinned back at me and shrugged his jacket into place, so damn sure I wouldn't start something in public.

Fingers digging into his shoulder, I leaned in and whispered, "*Cukkomd*." The spellword poured in through his ear, straight to the part of his human brain that was hard-wired to answer the old words. My friend Cocky Steve was now putty in my hands. "Don't talk. Follow me."

I threw my arm around Steve's loose shoulders, tossed a smile to the folks now grumbling and moving on, disappointed they hadn't gotten their Macy's brawl, and guided my new friend toward the restrooms.

We had company in the men's washrooms. Steve stood dull-eyed and dopey beside me as I waited for the stalls to vacate, using the good old-fashioned eyes-on glare to get the guys hustling.

Alone with Steve, I said, "*Hurzd*" to hold the main door closed. I glanced around the polished tiled walls. No cameras.

"So, here's how it's going to be, Steve. Mind if I call you Steve?"

He shook his head, looking somewhat startled. He was probably wondering why he wasn't fighting me and why all of this was playing out without his participation.

"Yeah, compulsion, it blows. Trust me, I know. But you ran, so that makes you a suspicious target. Then there's the little deal you did with the sorceress back there." His dopey eyes widened. "Yeah, her. All that usually wouldn't be enough for me to throw the command whammy on you, but unfortunately, the trick you did with the napkin... That's what caught my eye. So..." I leaned against the sink next to him. "Tell me all about that spell you cast when the sorceress turned her back."

His jaw worked, pale lips puckering. He tried to hold the words back, but while I had a grip on his mind and body, he wasn't winning this one.

"Minor spell. Tracking." He struggled, trembling. Poor bastard.

"You're tracking the sorceress?" I asked, needing confirmation.

He nodded.

"Why?"

"To find the Soul Eater." And there we go... the truth shall out.

"What soul eater?" I tested, feigning ignorance. It wasn't that hard.

"Sebek-kuh says there's one in the city. The sorceress is known to work with it."

It? Ouch. "What does this Sebek-kuh want with the Soul Eater?"

"I don't know."

"Is that the truth?"

"Yes."

"Are you lying? You wouldn't lie to me, would you, Steve?"

"No. No... Why... What... I don't know why I'm here. I shouldn't be talking to you. He's waiting."

"Who's waiting? Sebek-kuh?"

He nodded.

"You're meeting him?"

"Yes. I was supposed to cast the spell and go straight back to him."

I smiled and slapped nervous-wreck Steve on the back. "Well, let's not keep Mister Sebek-kuh waiting."

❧

MY NEW FRIEND, STEVE, WORKED ADMINISTRATION FOR Macy's, giving him personnel access throughout the building. He kindly agreed to take me on a tour of the basement where Mister Sebek-kuh was due to meet him in delivery bay 32B.

Refrigerated trailer units idled in their bays. Macy's back-end staff pushed wrapped and stacked trolleys from inside the trailers, making enough noise and commotion to distract them from Steve and me as we strolled by.

I told Steve to carry on as though I wasn't there, and he did exactly that, swaggering up to Bay 32, where a guy in a gray hoodie and matching pants waited.

Using some stacked yogurts as cover, I gave Sebek-kuh a casual once-over. He stood hunched over, his shoulders pulled in, his back bowed. From a distance, he looked frail, as though a strong gust of wind might blow him over. I wasn't buying it.

"Did you mark her?" Sebek-kuh asked, his voice a papery wheeze. I barely caught the words over the din of delivery vehicles.

"Yes."

"She didn't see?"

"No." Steve's shoulder twitched. My compulsion still had its hooks in him, but the cocky bastard was putting up a fight and trying to shove my control off him like someone trying to wipe off cobwebs. He had some skill, this one. Given enough time, he might even work free of me, but Steve wasn't my problem.

Sebek-kuh was laughing. At least I thought that was the rasping sound he was making. "Good, good," he exhaled.

I couldn't get a good look beneath the hood, but I'd seen enough possessed people over the decades to recognize a demon when I saw one, especially one that had spent too long hiding inside its host, rotting him from the inside out. I could smell the taint of its soul, like a cloud of diesel smoke.

"You have done as I asked. Now for your reward..." Sebek-kuh extended a pale, gnarled hand. His twiglike fingers clutched something that gave off the same foul sensation as his being.

I stepped out from behind the yogurts. "*Get behind me.*"

Steve obeyed and scooted around me, twitching and mumbling. I'd have to release him soon or risk permanent damage.

"I hear you're looking for the Soul Eater?"

Sebek-kuh lifted his face. Fluorescent lights pooled in his sunken eyes and glistened off his pearly white teeth behind tight, desiccated lips. He resembled something an archaeologist might dig up, and beneath the oily taint of his soul, he smelled of baked clay and hot stone.

"Soul Eater?" His lips pulled up at their corners, cracking his cheeks.

"In the flesh, which is more than I can say for you." I stopped a few feet in front of him. He had the wall at his back and on his left. His only exit, if he decided to bolt, was to my left, alongside the trucks. He only looked like he was one breath away from death. "All you had to do was pick up the phone. These days, every god and their enemies have me on their friends list."

"You would listen...?"

I screwed up my nose and pretended to think on it, noticing the camera blinking down at me from the corner. "Listen to a demon? No."

I didn't have Alysdair—I really needed to start the whole coat-and-sword gig again—so the unfortunate demon would be checking out the old-fashioned way, Soul Eater style. He still had eyes, even if they were weeping pus. Not long ago, I might have shied away from devouring a soul like his. These days, I wasn't as fussy. He shouldn't have been in my city.

"I came for you... *Mokarakk Oma.* For the Dark One who walks with you."

The Dark One was Shu, obviously. And I was done listening to lying demons. I checked the camera again.

Whether knowingly or by accident, Sebek-kuh stood beneath it, likely in its blind spot.

"I need your help, *Mokarakk Oma*. I need—"

A blade of light erupted from his foul guts, jolting the demon's hijacked body as though he'd been shocked with ten thousand volts. What little blood left in him oozed from the wound. The blade jerked, stuck in his ribs, and then cut clean through, opening the body from gut to gullet. The body collapsed in on itself and slumped in a heap of awkward body parts and leaking fluids.

Isis blinked at me innocently. "Were you in the middle of something?" She twisted her wrist, vanishing the blade, and planted her hand on her hip. Wearing a conservative green pantsuit and cream jacket, she'd toned down the goddess routine, but she still carried a luminous glow that would have any nearby human swooning in her presence.

"Holy shit," Steve gasped.

Isis flicked a finger at my temporary friend. "Rephrase."

"I—I... My god. It's true. You're, y-you—"

"So dull." She rolled her eyes and clicked her fingers. Steve was gone. Vanished, just like the blade. I didn't have the heart to ask where he'd gone, but I suspected Steve might wake up with no memory of the last twenty-four hours—if he was lucky. If he wasn't lucky, he might not wake up at all.

"Isis," I said carefully. The camera blinked in the corner, but I suspected her natural brilliance was blinding its lens.

"You didn't get my note?"

"Note?" I asked even more carefully. I had gotten her note asking for my help and mentioning something along the lines of how she knew "who I was." I burned her note right after reading it. That had been two weeks ago.

She stepped over Sebek-kuh's crumpled and rapidly decaying body, bringing her almost nose to nose with me. I wasn't backing down, even as my heart thudded hard and heavy and every instinct demanded I drop to a knee and bow my head. The sounds of the real world faded beneath the spell her beauty wove. I wasn't immune to her, and wishing I were didn't change a damn thing. Power throbbed around her in a warm, tempting caress. She was the Goddess of Light, of the Sky, Queen of Gods. Compared to her, I was a cockroach she could crush under her heel.

Paper crumpled in my hand. I frowned down at it, preferring to look there than into her eyes where I'd fall into that scorpion trap. "What's this?"

"Tickets. The flight to London Heathrow leaves at ten p.m. From there, you will take a connecting flight to Cairo. If you don't, I will tell my husband how you have, on numerous occasions, attempted to seduce me."

I tried to swallow but found my mouth dry and throat tight. "I'm not going back to Egypt."

"Oh dear, it appears as though you believe you have a choice. Silly, delusional Soul Eater."

I stuffed the tickets back in her hand, giving her the smallest shove. It was all I could do, but it gave me enough momentum to turn. "I'm not going. Tell Osiris you were hot in the sack, but I've had better."

She wouldn't do it. No way. If she were going to play the Osiris card, she'd have used it by now.

"Oh? My darling husband?"

I spun. She'd manifested a phone and was holding it against her ear. "There's something I must tell you—"

One stride in her direction and she showed me the lock screen. She hadn't made the call, but my hammering heart and the cold sweat down my back had me rethinking my decision. "You're insane."

"Blasphemy."

"Blasphemy? Peaches, I'm just warming up. I don't care if you're the goddess of the fucking past, present, and future.

I'm not going back to that godsforsaken city. Find some other schmuck."

"Ace Dante..." There was power in the way she said my name—not my real name, but the manufactured one, the superficial mask—as though she could tear it all away and reveal the truth of me beneath. "You have questions. You saw impossible things in the Twelve Gates—"

"How do you know that?"

"Because I know what you are, and I'll tell you everything. But first, you must go to Cairo."

Cairo, Egypt. The land that time forgot. The land the gods sundered. The land the sands devoured. "Fine. These had better be first class." I snatched the tickets back. "Why am I going to Cairo?"

"I'll tell you once we have arrived."

"Wait." *No, no, no.* Please, by Sekhmet, tell me I'd misheard her. "We?"

A smooth, knowing smile brightened her face. "Osiris will never know."

CHAPTER 2

Shukra looked up from her desk. It was one of those rare occasions when she left the door open so she could see me coming and spring whatever trap she'd set for me that morning. Her lips twitched into what passed for her usual snarl, and then she noticed the Goddess of Light behind me. Shu's smile froze, along with the rest of her face. Nothing good ever came from Isis visiting our offices. Shu knew this, and behind that mask, her whip-sharp mind would be racing through all the catastrophic motives for Isis dropping by.

I could have called ahead to warn her, but then I wouldn't have gotten to see Shu speechless. It was a marvelous thing.

Isis came to a silent halt a few steps inside the office. She wasn't glowing, and she'd toned down her blinding beauty. She appeared as nothing more than a businesswoman inspecting Shu's desk with a mildly inquisitive smile. That smile was a portent of doom. When gods smile, someone is about to suffer.

Shu placed her pen down, blinked once, and gingerly leaned back in her chair, making no sudden movements. "By

Isis, all that has been, that is, or shall be. My queen, welcome." She bowed her head, aware that if she said the wrong thing, she might lose it.

Osiris didn't want me—and by extension, Shukra—dead. Her death would be an inconvenience; mine would throw a giant wrench into Isis's plotting. The goddess couldn't set me up as her scapegoat if I was dead. Thoth's murder, the prophecy that someone's son would kill Osiris, Ammit's death—all fingers pointed at me, thanks to Isis. But I'd caught her in her lies.

"We're going to Cairo," I told Shu, throwing on some fake glee.

Her dark complexion paled to a wheat-like color. Her hands—cradled on her desktop—trembled. But not from fear. Anubis was the only thing Shukra feared. Those tremors came from the anger warming Shu's veins. Had we shared a telepathic connection, she'd be ranting and raging about the bitch-goddess pulling our strings and how getting between Osiris and Isis would get us killed. I'd get it all in the ear later, but in Isis's presence, Shukra swallowed her objections. "That's... wonderful?"

Isis swiped her fingertips along the edge of Shu's desk and drifted around the room. She admired Shu's framed hieroglyphs and scanned the various files. She moved like a snake, slow, methodical, and at her leisure.

Shu's dark eyes flicked questioningly to me. I waved her off with a small cutting gesture. Everything would be fine, so long as we didn't rile up the goddess. Whatever Isis wanted me to do, it would be over in a few days, and we'd be back in New York, picking up the cases we'd dropped in the meantime. No harm done. Easy.

"Pack a bag," I told Shu. "We leave tonight."

Shu rose to her feet.

"Oh, there's no need for that." Isis turned, tossed a golden locket and chain onto Shukra's desk, and spoke a single word. "*Amcruka.*" *Enclose.*

The locket exploded in a blast of light. I flinched away from the sudden blanching whiteness of Isis's power, but as quickly as the light had filled the room, it vanished, taking Shukra with it.

"Now the sorceress is a carry-on." Isis picked up the locket and threw it at me.

I snatched it out of the air. Hot metal burned my palm, and my only thought was how I didn't want to be within the sorceress's spell range when she was free.

Isis's smile had turned toxic. "Will the Soul Eater miss his pet sorceress? I didn't realize you two were so close. How *beastly*."

She could have bought another ticket instead of trapping Shukra, but Isis no more saw the sorceress as a person than she would a river beast. There was no point in arguing. It was done.

I dropped the locket into my coat pocket, keeping all the things I wanted to say firmly under my tongue.

"Come," Isis urged, already striding out of the office.

"I have appointments to cancel—"

She waved a hand. "Have the cat organize your diary."

"Cat left."

"The cripple, then." Isis paused at the end of the hallway and turned. As she did, she loosed a fragment of her power. The true goddess bled through, bringing with it the weight of her timeless power. The office, the building, it all started to feel smaller, and there I was, trapped inside with the presence of a true goddess about to crush me. "Do not test me, Nameless One, or you will find yourself being shipped to Cairo as cargo."

She clicked her fingers and disappeared, leaving only the

echo of her words and the faint scent of warm orchids behind.

⁂

AN ARRAY OF ALCOHOLIC DRINKS ACCOMPANIED THE FIRST-class flight from London Heathrow to Cairo. I set myself the goal of sampling them all and settled in for four hours of cradling expensive whiskeys, hoping to catch some sleep before the plane touched down on Egyptian soil. Egypt had always been restless. Deep within the country's bedrock, were memories of how its gods had once ruled the worlds and how those same gods had lost it all. History tells us Egypt's wealth waned, its crops failed year after year, and its political power shrank. In the history books, Egypt's might didn't burn out; it was snuffed out over many, many centuries. History is wrong. Egypt didn't die a slow, inevitable death; it was slaughtered. When gods go to war, worlds tremble beneath their feet. Egypt had borne the brunt of the great sundering. Vast cities, glorious temples, and verdant lands had all been annihilated, leaving nothing behind but dust, sand, and ruins.

I didn't want to go back.

I didn't want to remember.

Hence the whiskey. I'd have preferred vodka, but considering how this journey had the makings of a nightmare, I'd have drunk paint thinner.

I sensed Isis before seeing her. As much as she could wrap her power up and hide it away, my survival instincts were attuned to nearby gods and goddesses with murderous impulses. Isis poured her entire presence into the first-class booth next to mine. She hadn't joined me on the transatlantic flight. I'd started hoping she'd missed the flight altogether. I should have known my respite wouldn't last.

I downed the whiskey and hailed the attendant for another.

"Slumming it with the peons?" I asked Isis without looking at her. In the corner of my eye, I saw her soft hands run over her thighs, smoothing out any creases in her expensive black satin pants. "Or checking up on me?"

The attendant delivered my fresh glass of whiskey. I'd probably had enough to drink, but the edges of reality were still too sharp and the alcohol hadn't dulled the sense of dread hanging around like bad cologne. And now I had a visitor. Maybe I could drink myself unconscious to be rid of her?

Taking a generous sip, I looked over at Isis and immediately wished I hadn't. A multicolored silk hijab framed her exquisitely beautiful face. *Beautiful* didn't touch the vision of her. Dark eyes and long lashes made sultry promises, and when she turned her gaze on me, I found myself wishing Shu were here to slap some much-needed sense into me. Osiris instilled respect and devotion in people, but his wife was made of finer things. Many souls had fallen into her trap over millennia. Isis was among the few still worshipped by a handful of fools. Once, she had been a queen, a goddess, a mother, a symbol of brightness and all that was righteous. But like her husband, the years after the sundering had twisted her into a cruel imitation of herself. As vicious as she was, that didn't stop the human parts of me from appreciating the timeless art of her design. *Goddess of Light. Do. Not. Touch.* By Sekhmet, how was I supposed to resist the temptation that was Isis over however many days this would take? I'd never had much self-control.

"I have not returned since the sundering," she said with a forlorn sigh.

I stared at the back of the booth in front of me, willing my heart to stop racing.

"I could not bring myself to see it," she added.

I knew what she felt because I felt it too. The land we had loved had become a parody of itself. Thousands of tourists trampled over sacred grounds, touched temple reliefs and crumbling ancient art with their oily fingers, and bought cheap papyrus with their names scrawled in hieroglyphs, as though the death of the greatest civilization that had ever existed was a cosmic joke bought for a few Egyptian pounds.

It wasn't the whiskey giving me nausea. "Then why are you going back now?"

She didn't answer, choosing instead to stew in silence. It was all an act. Isis was beyond emotions such as sadness for a long-dead world. She was a goddess, crowned queen of New York, the Light of Life. This sadness was make-believe, probably to soften me up and have me dutifully do her bidding. I might have once—a long time ago—but not after she'd tried to seduce me, framed me for killing two gods, and possibly set in motion the kind of prophecy that would get her husband killed and my insides scattered throughout the underworld. Add to that the frivolous murders she and her husband had compelled me to commit. Yeah, she could take her pseudo-sadness and shove it where her eternal light didn't shine.

"Archaeologists discovered a tomb in the Valley of the Queens," she finally answered. "They are excavating as we speak."

I didn't need to see her face to see the twist of her lips. Her disgust was clear in the abrasive edge to her voice. Few gods appreciated human "experts" picking through the remains of the past.

"There are items inside that the archaeologists must not disturb," she said.

"What items?"

Her long, heated look could have shriveled souls. Clearly, I'd asked the wrong question.

I tried another angle. "Whose tomb is it?"

"A minor noble," she replied, looking around the cabin as though this conversation bored her.

She knew every tomb in those ancient valleys, including those that curious professors had yet to plunder. She hadn't plucked me out of my nine-to-five to visit a minor tomb and retrieve trinkets for her. She could have done that herself or asked a devoted fan or her husband. Whatever was going on here, it wasn't minor, and she didn't want Osiris knowing.

I couldn't tell Osiris about this trip without the god losing his shit. He was already aware that I might have, once or twice, imagined his wife and me in situations too hot for YouTube. If he discovered my vacation with Isis, he'd turn my testicles into shriveled cufflinks and wear them to his next charity gala.

"You aren't going to tell me anything of use, are you?" I asked.

"You will find out soon enough."

"Or you could save me the surprise?"

"Do not worry yourself with details, *Ace Dante*."

My name on her lips sounded entirely too wrong. Ace Dante was a lie. "When do I get to learn *who I am*?"

"When we're done." She lifted her hand and summoned an attendant. The same woman who'd served me approached Isis. "Fetch me a drink," the goddess ordered.

The attendant, for some reason, looked at me as though I had something to do with Isis's attitude.

"She thinks she's a goddess," I muttered, smiling my overly bright grin.

"We have a selection of spirits or champagne—"

"Only the best," Isis replied and then added a sensual, "Please."

I almost choked on my whiskey. I wouldn't have believed the word *please* was in Isis's vocabulary if I hadn't heard it myself. The attendant dutifully hurried off to fetch her drink, and Isis eyed the woman hungrily. I needed to remember that Isis had been playing her games for thousands of years. I no more knew her than I knew the elusive Amun Ra.

I sank low in my seat and vowed to keep my head down and my wits about me so I could get this secret vacation over with. If luck was on my side, I might even come out the other side with all my body parts intact.

CHAPTER 3

The cabin door opened, and Egypt's oven-hot air blasted in, stealing the breath from my lungs. Inside the terminal, the suffocating sensation didn't ease until I'd shuffled through immigration, alongside all the other passenger-cattle. Finally stepping from Cairo International onto the pick-up/drop-off area, I dragged in a long, deep breath and tasted baked stone, traffic fumes, and hot dust. A local man made a grab for my bags. He'd try to ferry me toward a waiting tourist bus a few hundred yards away and demand an extortionate tip. I must have been away too long for him to mistake me for a tourist.

"Emshi, ibn kalb," I said, reeling off a mildly offensive term in Arabic and driving the point home with a touch of soul-eater glare.

He scurried off, muttering, *"Ana aasif, aasif..."* already searching for his next unwitting victim.

Sweat dripped down my neck, gluing my shirt to my back. It would take a few days to acclimatize. Hopefully, I'd be back on a plane before then.

Isis strode from the terminal exit, designer sunglasses

shielding her eyes. She looked as though she had just walked off a photo shoot for *Elite Traveler* magazine and captured the gaze of every man and woman loitering nearby. She ignored them and me, stopped at the curb, and lifted her hand. A sleek, white Mercedes peeled free from the traffic and prowled to a stop along the curb. The chauffeur, a young Egyptian man with an eager smile and a knitted skull cap, hopped out and opened the door for Isis. He left me to haul my own bags to the trunk.

Isis didn't speak a word as we carved through Cairo's traffic out of the city, but behind those shades, she was watching the modern buildings reel by. Once the city gave way to desert, she fell into an immobile, silent mood. A connecting flight to Luxor would have been easier, or she could have clicked her fingers and appeared wherever she needed to be, so the six hours spent staring at sand probably had a reason, but it was beyond me. I dozed and only once fell asleep, but I woke with a start, my head filled with dreams of blood-red sand and hungry shadows.

Her driver dropped us off inside a gated luxury resort. Hotel staff busied around Isis like ants around their queen, and I was again left trailing behind. The cavernous foyer shone with polished marble, glass, and gold. The pretentious interior should have been hideous, but the designers had erred on the right side of subtle, playing with warm light and gold accents to create something that plucked on my memories of Duat—home.

Isis disappeared while I checked in and headed to my room, taking the pressure of her presence with her. For the first time in what felt like a lifetime of traveling, I breathed freely. I had a lot that I wanted to tell the goddess, but over the years, I'd learned that demanding answers out of her was the wrong way to go about things. I could try prying them out over the next few days, without an Osiris-shaped shadow looming over us. A dangerous game, Shukra would have said, but one I was equipped to play. While Isis wanted something from me, I held all the cards.

I wandered through my ridiculously huge multi-room apartment. Who needed blue mood lighting around a bath? If my room was this luxurious, Isis's was probably a palace. If everything went well, I'd never see it. *Goddess of Light. Do. Not. Touch.* That was the only rule I couldn't break while in Egypt. An easy-enough task. She was, after all, as crazy as a sack of cobras.

My feet had found their way to the windows. A couple of miles beyond the hotel gates, the ancient Karnak temple glowed in the dark. I could sense its song, the constant background hum warm and inviting. Impressive as a ruin today, it had been astonishing during its prime—a riot of color and light and celebration. Now, time had gnawed at its edges, but the huge stone pylons still held power.

I opened the window, letting the super-heated evening air pour in.

"*Rarru*," I whispered. *Hello*. Unlike Duat's Halls of Judgment, Karnak didn't answer. But it was there, slumbering, still alive and waiting. I wouldn't be able to stay away for long.

I leaned against the window frame and relaxed the Ace Dante persona, easing some of my magic through. The air took it and swept it out of the window, spreading it far like pollen on the breeze. Stretched far and thin, I could lose myself. I breathed it back in. I was a fool for believing coming back to Egypt would be simple. The land might be dead to most, its truth hidden in myths and legends, but to me, the magic beat through the earth like a leviathan's heavy heart. And it would be beating for Isis too. She'd sense it more keenly and remember her power from *before*. Remember the might of the gods and how thousands upon thousands had worshipped her. If these lands tugged on me, they had to be crying out to her.

I pushed away from the window, turned my back on Karnak and its temptation, showered, dressed in a baggy shirt and the only pair of loose linen pants I owned, and headed through the hotel to the pool area. Light bloomed around the gardens, bleeding through leaning palm trees. Nothing obscene, just subtle touches of light here and there. Isis stood at the far end, at the top of limestone steps, looking toward Karnak, though swaying palms blocked the view. We were the only people outside, besides the occasional waiter checking that each chair and blade of grass was in the correct place. I could see why Isis liked it here; the attentive service must have reminded her of how things used to be.

"Are you ready to tell me why we're here?" I asked as I approached, not wanting to startle her.

Her shoulders stiffened. "I knew it would be difficult, but I..." Isis's voice cracked. Nothing about her ever cracked. It never wavered, or failed, or showed any weakness.

I dug my hands into my pants pockets, curling Shu's locket around my fingers. *She's a viper. Just because this place is getting to her, it doesn't change a damn thing.*

"You must feel it," she murmured, turning her head so the soft garden lighting spilled over her golden skin, highlighting the downturn of her lips and the too-bright glisten in her eyes.

Enough. "I didn't come here to reminisce, Your Highness. I don't want to be here at all. So let's cut the bullshit and get on with whatever you've dragged my ass out here for."

She pushed her hijab back from her face and let the silk pool over her small shoulders. When had she started looking small? Those pretty eyes of hers glistened with magic, because it couldn't be tears. Isis didn't do those.

I pulled Shu's locket free and dangled it between us.

"Bring Shukra back." I needed that damn sorceress here to stop me from doing something stupid—multiple stupid things in multiple ways.

Isis's eyes narrowed on the spinning locket. "She is an abomination. Why would you want her here?"

"Why don't you?"

A shrug. "I do not care either way. Condemned demons do not feature in my thoughts at all."

"Good, then bring her back and continue not to care."

"No."

I gritted my teeth, aware I was already making demands, but I had my limits and she was getting close to the edge. "You assume I won't tell Osiris any of this, but I could."

Her eyes hardened. "That would be... *unwise*."

"So don't make me post an update on Facebook. '*Having a fantastic time in Luxor with the Goddess of Light.*' Bring Shu back and I promise I won't tag Osiris."

A tiny ungodlike snarl pulled at her grimace. "Who do you think you are to threaten me in this manner?" Oh yes, this was more like the Isis I knew. Rage burned away whatever tears had swum in her eyes, and I was back in familiar territory: an angry Isis, and me pushing her buttons.

"I'm the Soul Eater, Ace Dante, Nameless One, and the last time I checked, Godkiller. So bring Shukra back. Do it or this expedition goes viral."

She lifted her chin. "Nobody speaks to me like this and none have for millennia. You are a base creature, a monster with no name. You should not be here, breathing my air, walking this same earth. I am Light. You are the dark. You should be under the Halls with your disgusting river beasts. Why my husband allowed you a seat in the weighing chambers, why he allowed Ammit to take you in, to lift you up to the heights of the gods, I wish I knew. You are a scourge, *Mokarakk Oma*."

I smiled at the venom in her words, letting each insult drip right off. "Bring Shukra back. Now."

Isis ripped the locket from my grip and tossed it into the pool. It splashed into the still water, sending ripples lapping at the edges, and sashayed to the bottom.

"You and your demon lover can rot in *mu moka* until the End of All Things."

Say what you will about me, but I sure know how to piss off goddesses.

Isis clicked her fingers and vanished as a blast of white light boiled half the pool dry and birthed a hissing, spitting ball of furious demon sorceress. Shu climbed over the pool's edge, dripping water and seething so much I could feel the heat from where I stood. Silent lightning crackled across the cloudless night sky. Okay then...

Shukra swept her wet hair back, lifted her chin, straightened her waterlogged fur coat (ideal for New York's windy streets, but not so good for the desert) and glared daggers at me.

There's no right thing to say to someone who had a goddess trap them in a locket for over twenty-four hours and almost six thousand air miles. I smiled, careful to hide my relief over having her back. "It could have been worse."

She lifted a finger and pressed her lips together, fighting to keep from speaking. A curse bubbled on her tongue. I couldn't see it, but I could feel it in the power rushing toward her.

She blinked a few times, noticing the pool, then the palm trees, and lastly the heat, and figured out she wasn't in New York anymore. A deep breath shuddered in. She held it, and only when she had herself under control did she say, "I am going to the bar." Each word was clipped, holding back demon growls. "If anyone so much as comes near me, I'll dice them up and mail them to their closest living relative."

"Shu—"

Boots squelching, she walked away like she might murder the next living thing to cross her path and saluted her middle finger over her shoulder.

I didn't care that she was pissed at me. She was back, and with Shukra at my side, there was a chance I might survive Isis and Egypt.

CHAPTER 4

"You smell like hot sand and baked rock," Shu grunted by way of greeting.

"I visited Karnak last night," I replied, keeping my voice low so it wouldn't carry across the cavernous hotel lobby. Wandering around ancient temples was a fantastic way to get arrested and thrown into an Egyptian prison cell. The Egyptian authorities didn't screw around. They couldn't afford to have tourists stumble in the dark, liable to get kidnapped and ransomed or shot, or have them accidentally scrub out ancient hieroglyphs that had survived over thousands of years just fine. But I wasn't any tourist, nor was I normal.

"Did Karnak say hello?" Shu asked.

"No." I didn't elaborate. I'd tried waking Karnak, just enough to see what, if any, power remained, but the old temple stubbornly lay dormant.

"Maybe you don't have enough juice."

I hadn't devoured much of anything in weeks. My *juice* was low. "Maybe." But this land was potent, and it had started stirring parts of me I preferred to keep buried. It wasn't a mystery how bad shit happened when I got twitchy. I'd hoped Karnak might help settle my nerves, but it hadn't. If anything, it had made it worse.

Shu tapped her sandals impatiently against the floor. "Bitch is late."

"It's Isis. Time revolves around her."

Shu plucked at her long-sleeved beige blouse. Her white linen pants and light blouse complemented her dark skin. She looked marginally less likely to stab someone in the heart than when she'd crawled from the pool.

"Nice hat," Shu said, making it sound like, *You're a dumbass.*

I flicked the rim of my Indiana Jones fedora hat, bartered from a market stall on my way back from Karnak. "You'll want one just like it once you're in the midday sun."

I had on the loose pants and shirt from the night before, hence why Shu could smell the temple on me. Isis wouldn't notice. She didn't care what I did or said or wore, so long as I came to heel like a good little mutt.

"If you wore your true skin, you wouldn't get burned."

"Oh sure, turning into a storm made of shadow and ash that happens to consume souls wouldn't terrify the locals at all."

She shrugged. "You weren't always this milky, mocha-skinned New Yorker."

"I wasn't always a lot of things. Time changes everything."

"Not everything."

There were many layers beneath her meaning in the way she spoke. Time had changed me, and her, and the gods—those who remained. The rest, the gods who'd taken their slumber, didn't change and neither did those like Anubis, who continued to rule the underworld. Sometimes, in the dead of night, when even New York was quiet, I wondered about those sleeping gods and what they'd do when—if they returned.

Isis emerged from inside the hotel, sunglasses on. She wore billowing white pants that looked more like a skirt than pants and a green silk blouse. The same hijab hid her dark hair and shielded part of her face from prying eyes. If she was trying not to stand out, she was doing it wrong. The hotel staff and tourists all turned to her. What would they do if they knew Isis walked among them?

"Stop me from saying something that'll get me killed," Shu mumbled.

I'd been about to ask her the same. "We survived the Chicago outfit," I said through a fake smile as Isis glanced our way, fixing us in her sights. "Survived Osiris, wars, murderous plots, scuttled ships, slave traders, arctic winters, enraged demons, angry gods, superstitious mobs, vengeance, and Anubis's justice. We can survive Isis."

Shu swallowed hard.

"Come." Isis sauntered by, waving us into motion behind her.

Shu rolled her eyes, and we set off after Isis. Outside, the open-top Jeep that would take us to the Valley of the Queens waited.

Ta-Set-Neferu, THE PLACE OF BEAUTY, TODAY KNOWN AS the Valley of the Queens, had once been a verdant valley. The nearby Nile, a network of farm troughs, careful management and Osiris's life-rich touch had kept it green. Now, as the Jeep pulled to a halt, dust wafted into the air. Sunlight beat down, baking the sandstone rock faces and turning the steep valley into a furnace.

Isis climbed out of the vehicle and surveyed the section of road that split off toward Hatshepsut's temple. Her hijab protected her mouth and nose from the dust, while her sunglasses shielded her eyes, though she needn't have bothered. Not a grain of dirt touched her. Shu and I, on the other hand... I'd seen camels wear less desert than us two.

Before returning, I'd known what remained of the valleys, but standing on those remains while my memories superimposed the old lush scenes over the barren landscape shifted reality around me, taking my balance with it. Streams of tourists poured into the valley to pay their respects to the dead. They would come and leave offerings or beg for help from the pharaohs—who, in death, were granted godlike status. They weren't gods, of course. The pharaohs had died like all mortals. Some had carried god-given favors with them to the underworld—borrowed magic—while others weren't as lucky, but all had been weighed and dealt with accordingly, unless they'd been unlucky enough to cross me. I'd eaten the sweetest ones.

"If you two are finished staring into nothing," Shu grumbled, stomping past me, "let's move."

Isis didn't spare us a glance or acknowledge Shukra. She started up the winding path in her own time, and by her easy strides, she didn't appear to be in any hurry. Old gods always struggle with time management. She passed Shukra as though the sorceress was nothing more than the dust she walked through.

I trudged up to Shu. "What are the chances this will be over by lunch?"

"Same as me getting a pay raise." Shukra shooed a few flies away from her face and squinted after Isis. "Is she always this icy?"

"Be grateful." I didn't elaborate, which earned me a scowl. Shu and I could talk back at the hotel bar, but here, I understood Isis's need for silence. Despite the invading tourists, grumbling tour buses, and chattering tour guides, this was a sacred place. The earth hummed with slumbering power, fragmented and scattered over time until all that was left might as well have been dust in the wind, but it was there, like the dying embers of a collapsed inferno. The weight of terrible loss pulled on my damaged soul. I kept my head down and marched on, climbing to where the valley narrowed and the tombs collected.

There was little to show the tombs on the outside, just steps down what appeared to be random holes in the ground. Each hole was marked by an information board. The Valley of the Queens didn't attract the same volume of tourists as the Valley of the Kings. With too much to see, tourists often overlooked the queens for Tutankhamen's desiccated body and Hatshepsut's sprawling temple.

I tried not to sneer at the few ruddy-skinned tourists ambling along, snapping selfies with their cells. Shu didn't bother restraining herself and scared off a few with a look and a snarl.

Isis continued her relentless march up the hill, and I started to wish we'd ventured here at night. There weren't many tourists around, but it would have been much easier to rob a tomb in the dark. This was probably a recce.

Isis stopped at the information board that definitely didn't mark a newly discovered tomb, but the excavation going on behind us was. A simple make-do cordon of tape and stones marked the hole in the ground, but no one was home. Tourists wandered by, more interested in the open tombs than the depression in the ground.

"The archaeology teams work at dawn and dusk," Isis said. It was the first time she'd spoken since leaving the hotel. She didn't look behind us, and with those shades guarding her eyes and her hijab hiding her mouth, I couldn't read her expression. "Go inside. You don't have long."

I scanned the tomb openings and tried to orientate myself with who was buried here, not that it would do any good.

Tombs were often forgotten and reopened, moved, or dug over. There was no order to their locations, but this end of the valley held some of the oldest known resting places. Most archaeologists had believed this branch was all tapped out. Someone had gotten lucky to find the capping stone and recognize it for what it was.

"Are you going to tell me what I'm looking for?" I asked, pretending to admire the information board next her. "Or shall I grab armfuls of gold and hope for the best?"

"A skull."

"A skull?"

She tilted her head. "Leave anything else behind."

I could hide a skull under my shirt. Trying to smuggle a desiccated two-thousand-year-old corpse out of the Valley of the Queens would have been interesting.

"Nothing else?" I asked, keeping my frustration from my voice. All this way to grab a skull? She didn't need me for this. She didn't even need to be here. A few phone calls to the dig team and she could have gotten her skull shipped via UPS. "No trinkets, jewelry, or finger bones?"

"Nothing."

"Are there more remains inside? More than one skull to pick from?"

"Just retrieve the skull," she snapped, white teeth flashing.

Shukra caught my eye and clearly believed this excursion was a waste of our time; we could have been back in New York, breathing in diesel soot instead of sand.

I hopped over the flimsy tape barrier and confidently descended the timber ladder, feigning a right to be there. Shu followed me down and stooped beside me. The dig team hadn't fully cleared the chamber floor of seasonal flood debris, and much of it was still banked against the walls. My hat brushed the tomb roof. I plucked it off and ruffled my hair, shaking dust free. Ahead, a string of work lights illuminated a long hall and more... This was no insignificant tomb. Hieroglyphs covered the walls and ceiling, without an inch of surface to spare. Time had worn away what had once been a fantastic display, but much of the burial scenes were intact.

"This is nuts, even for her bitchiness," Shu remarked as she brushed dust from her hands.

I started forward. "Check the cartouches for a name. I want to know whose tomb we're in and why its occupant has Isis tied up in knots."

Shu hung back and examined the hieroglyphs as I strode on, sucking hot, dusty air through my teeth.

"I'm not seeing any curses," Shu announced. Her voice bounced around the tomb's interior, echoing left and right. "Don't feel anything either."

That was something. Some tombs had been cursed to deter robbers. Most had had their curses broken as easily as kicking open a lock, but some, like Tutankhamen's, had carried real bite behind them.

"Huh?" Shu said.

I pulled up short of the end of the hall, where it appeared to split off in two directions, and turned at the question in Shu's voice.

"Someone scrubbed out the cartouches."

I could just make out Shu's shadow on a wall. The rest of her was tucked around a chamber corner. "All of them?" I called.

"So far... Whoever's buried here, someone really, really didn't like them."

"*Kres*," I cursed. Erasing a name from inside a cartouche did more than scrub someone from history; it scrubbed them from the underworld too, destroying them in life and death. There wasn't another form of punishment that came close, besides me, naturally. It also meant I wouldn't discover whose tomb this was or whose skull I was about to steal for Isis.

Shu appeared, hunched over to keep her head from brushing the ceiling, and headed toward me. "You should have told Isis where to stick her little trip—"

A wave of rock poured into the chamber, blasting hot air down the passageway and engulfing Shukra. The dust cloud blasted over me. Grit pummeled my face and bit into my skin, and then it was over. The rumbling ceased. Pebbles tumbled. Rock settled. I blinked into the rolling clouds, eyes dry, and spotted Shu's shadowy outline. She coughed as she emerged from the dust, covered head to toe in powder-soft sand.

The work lights still glowed, so we weren't plunged into darkness, but the exit was blocked. Shu regarded the rockfall with a snort. "Egypt. The gift that keeps on giving."

I spat dust and sand to the side, wondering if the real reason Isis had brought us all the way out here was to bury Shu and me in a tomb. It wouldn't be the worst thing the gods had done to us.

"Could be worse," I spluttered.

"You need to stop saying that before I show you worse." Shu brushed by me and stalked off deeper into the tomb. "Since I'm stuck here with you, I'm taking the tour."

I let her go and eyed the rockfall. There was a slim chance the collapse had been natural, but I hadn't seen any cracks in the ceiling. My gut said Isis had just buried me alive, but what my gut didn't reveal was why. As I pushed into the tomb, the hallway narrowed and the old flood debris piled higher, squeezing out space. Shu's swearing bounced off the walls ahead. There was probably another way out. Possibly. If there wasn't, we'd find out how long a soul eater and a demon sorceress could survive without oxygen.

CHAPTER 5

"Why is Isis so hot for you?"

"Why wouldn't she be? I'm a prize catch." I grinned at Shukra's eye roll and continued shifting rocks away from a small opening into yet another chamber. We'd already passed through five others. Hours had slipped by. The tomb was a maze of chambers, ante-chambers, alcoves, and corridors, and there was no skull in sight.

"Isis never used to look twice at you. Now she's asking for favors and getting in your head and your pants." Shu chuckled, like the idea of Isis and me was ludicrous. I would have laughed right along with her if Isis hadn't been stalking my dreams every night. "So, what changed?"

Good question, but the answer wasn't. "Thoth. When I killed him, I set a bunch of Isis's godly games into motion."

Shu shifted her stones. In the low light, I could just make out her ever-cynical eyes and the gleam of sweat on her face. Her quiet preluded more questions, and stuck as we were, I couldn't escape them.

"The prophecy about a son killing a god?" she asked.

The son will sunder a king... I heard Isis saying those exact words, *remembered* it, but I couldn't recall from where or when. "Right. That prophecy." Shu had been there when I'd stabbed Alysdair through Thoth's chest. She'd heard the God of Law mention the prophecy. "Isis used Thoth to put into motion an alleged prophecy that will kill her husband. She can't do it herself because then she wouldn't be the Goddess of Light who loves her husband dearly, so she's using those around her, but mostly me. I know it, I just can't prove it."

"Prophecies." Shu snorted. "She believes in a godstruck priest's fantasy?"

I was sure Isis didn't believe in anything but herself. "Isis doesn't have to believe it as long as those around her do, including Thoth. She's making it happen, and she's got me buried up to my neck in it. All fingers point to me." I rocked back on my heels and counted down on my fingers. "I've got motive—I'd happily kill Osiris and the entire pantheon knows it—and I've got a rap sheet." More fingers fell. "Ammit, Thoth, it doesn't matter that I didn't technically kill them. It's all Isis's doing. She had Ammit killed, and she knew I'd lose it when I discovered the body and consume all the souls in that room. She convinced Thoth to kill himself by proxy. Plus, I'm not the most innocent soul. If Osiris dies, Isis gets to be the grieving wife and wear the crown, while I get to play pin the body part on the soul eater with Anubis for all eternity."

Even in the dark, Shu's glower was obvious. "Anubis weighed your heart against Ammit's murder. I doubted it, but the feather was clear. You're innocent."

"Innocent?" I chuckled dryly. That word didn't belong in the same sentence as my name. "So the feather's judgment was right for that crime. But I did kill Thoth, and I am despised everywhere I go in the underworld, with good reason. Isis set me up as the villain in her tragic love story.

Nobody will challenge her. It'd be like trying to convince everyone that Jafar was the real hero of *Aladdin*."

Shukra dug around more stones and shifted them out of the doorway. The only sound was the grinding of stones and our ragged breaths in the dark. We had plenty of air, for now, but I felt it thinning as I trawled it over my tongue.

"So Isis isn't trying to stop the prophecy; she's encouraging it?"

"Oh, she'll go to any lengths to be *seen* as the dutiful wife who's protecting her husband. Their love is *eternal,* and anyone who doubts that faces Osiris's wrath. But I know what she's doing, and she knows I know. Hence the come-ons, getting inside my head, dragging my ass out here, and probably why we're buried in a tomb."

"All this dancing around just to kill Osiris?" Shu heaved a large rock out of the way and dumped it behind her.

"He's the God of Rebirth. His brother, Seth, killed him once already. He doesn't die and stay dead without a lot of effort."

Debris in the blocked doorway crumbled. Shu backed up, and I kicked the rest of the rocks in, stirring up more dust. As it settled, a chamber opened beyond. A trickle of power hummed in the background, enough to confirm there was something worth finding here, and it was probably inside the stone sarcophagus sitting dead center in the room.

"You feel it? A curse?" I asked, referring to the power's background tickle.

"Could be."

As far sarcophagi went, this was one plain. More of a stone box than a vessel to travel the underworld. What few hieroglyphs remained mentioned a great builder, but no pharaoh.

I ran my hand over the markings. None flared to life. Whatever magic was left, it wasn't in the writing.

Crouching close, I read the inscriptions. The hieroglyphs depicted someone risen from poverty to a position of power.

"This tomb belongs to a man," I said, noticing the subtle accents on various scenes.

Shu took a closer look over my shoulder. "A man buried in the Valley of the Queens?"

"Some sarcophagi were moved over the thousands of years to keep them hidden from angry pharaohs and opportunistic robbers." I straightened to get a better look at the hieroglyphs on the walls, but the work lights ended in the hallway, filling the burial chamber with shadows. Alysdair's glow would have come in handy, but I'd left the sword back in the hotel room. "Can you spell a little light?"

Shu uttered a few words and cupped her hand in the air. Something long and thin wriggled in her palm. A *sruvurk*—glow worm—the kind that, in Shu's hands, could crawl up your nose and set your brain matter on fire. She tossed it into the air, where it flung out sticky silk and dangled from the tomb ceiling. Comfortable, it started glowing.

Light spilled over the hieroglyphs, revealing scenes of people bowing at his feet. "Looks like he was someone special... See here... He's depicted standing behind a woman... a pharaoh." Only a handful of female pharaohs had come to power, which narrowed it down considerably.

I ran my hands over several cartouches that had been chiseled away. Where the cuts ran deep, old magic throbbed like a festering wound. Some clues remained. Crooks and flails, and the upper and lower Egyptian crowns. "This man was Queen Hatshepsut's advisor. Ammit weighed his soul before my time in the Halls. She told me he'd been one of the lightest souls she'd ever weighed. The sarcophagus belongs to Senenmut."

Shu's eyes glowed brighter, the yellow in them bleeding

through. She recognized the name. "If I find his canopic jars, can I keep them?"

"No. We came for the skull." The brightness in her gaze sharpened. "Don't touch anything else."

"You're kidding, right?"

I gripped the edge of the sarcophagus lid and worked my fingers into a comfortable position. The stone felt *warm* under my touch. The latent magic, tentative and old, continued its soft pawing at my mind. "Serious as Tut's curse."

"Isis put me in a locket, dragged my ass out to a country as hot and filthy as Seth's armpit, and buried me in a tomb with you, and I don't get to keep any souvenirs?"

"Are you really arguing about this now?" I shoved the lid. The seal cracked, but the lid had barely moved.

"I'm taking a jar." She huffed, sounding more like a disgruntled teen than a demon sorceress of unknown origin.

"Shu, help me with this lid."

She locked her hands on the edge of the lid and pushed.

I braced my boots against the floor and heaved with her, shoving what felt like five tons of stone a millimeter. Then another.

"You're not taking a jar," I hissed. Canopic jars held a body's most valuable organs. In Shu's hands, a canopic jar holding just a fraction of someone as important as Senenmut was a biblical plague waiting to happen.

"I'm taking a jar," she hissed back.

"I'll tell Isis to put you back"—the lid jolted—"in the locket."

"I'll tell Osiris you've had Isis *all the human ways* and some ways that are definitely not human."

I laughed, knowing she wouldn't. Any punishment Osiris rained down on me was her punishment too. He'd kill anyone who delivered that message out of principle.

The sarcophagus lid jolted again and gasped millennia-old air. With it came a boiling mass of glistening black bodies, each the size of my hand. Scorpions. They were on me, pouring over my fingers and up my arms. Needle-like claws dug in. Pincers clicked. Stingers cocked.

Shu screamed. Her glowing worm died—probably eaten—plunging us into darkness.

"Hurzd!" The spellword shot from my lips, around a pincer, and slammed into the oncoming flood, freezing the scorpions and locking every single one down. But in the absolute blackness, I couldn't see them. I didn't *want* to see. The weight of their bodies clung to my clothes. There had to be hundreds—thousands—enough to make the strain of holding them shudder and twitch through my control.

I spat the scorpion off my lip. "Shu?"

"Here," she answered, voice tight.

"Light?"

After a few seconds, another glowing worm hovered in the air, illuminating the walls, a sarcophagus, and the ceiling, all covered in shiny-black scorpions. None moved. Beady eyes watched me, tails hooked over and pincers raised, waiting for my spellword to fail.

"I can burn them..." she whispered.

"And us." *And use up the rest of our oxygen.* I plucked several off my arm and tossed them into the ankle-deep layer covering the floor. Shu did the same, avoiding their hooked stingers. These weren't normal scorpions. Bigger and more aggressive, they'd come straight from the same place as the delightful sand-tunneling *vurk* that had recently terrorized a Long Island beach: my backyard, *mu moka.*

"I'm holding them," I told her and winced against the strain.

"For now." She yanked one from her hair and tossed it at a wall.

She was right to worry. I'd controlled a wave of snakes in Duat, but this ancient tomb wasn't Duat, and I didn't have the same power here as I did back home.

Inching forward, I leaned over the sarcophagus to get my first look inside. The mummy had shrunk in size, revealing the shocking decayed carcass of a once proud and substantial man. Skin had contracted and turned prune dark. The years had not been kind to Senenmut.

"Well, he's mostly intact." Four canopic jars were nestled against the corpse. I kept that knowledge to myself.

"No skull?"

"Give the sorceress a prize."

Senenmut's neck had been severed after the embalming process. There was a slim chance the archaeologists had gotten through the door, shifted the sarcophagus's lid, and taken the head, but considering the scorpion welcoming party, I doubted it. The skull had probably been taken *before* Senenmut was entombed—sometime a few thousand years ago, give or take a decade. Great.

My hold on the scorpions wavered, and they shifted, jerking forward, bodies creaking.

"Hurzd..." I strengthened the hold, but it wouldn't last. A magical backlash was already stalking me.

"Plan B." I headed for the doorway, grateful for solid shoes when the carapaces cracked like candy under my soles. Shu couldn't say the same about her sandals.

"Which is?"

"It's always the same. Run."

We didn't get far. Corridors switched back on themselves while others dug deeper into the earth. Shu kept her glow worm alive in her hand, illuminating walls that all looked the same. Round and around we went, with no exit in sight.

"We've been here before," I murmured.

In the sarcophagus chamber, now somewhere above us,

the scorpions pushed forward as one huge wave. I stumbled and reached for the wall just as they snapped free of my will. Razor-edged pain lashed through the inside of my skull.

Shukra spat a curse, rolled her shoulders, and deliberately shuffled off *human*, setting her eyes aflame with yellow light. "All right, then, barbeque bugs for dinner!"

"There has to be," I panted, dragging hot air through my teeth, "another way out."

Shu turned her palms up and faced the tide of oncoming thousands. "*Amun Ra, bae orr uk aeuir kesrs.*" Her voice dropped, adopting tones and hitches that didn't belong to human vocal cords. *"Sroms ka sra resrs, sra raos, sra amarsae, kerr ka vesr aeuir akkamka. Braosr kera emsu ka."*

I didn't know the spell, but she was invoking Ra's name, something few sorceresses were powerful enough to handle.

Fire opened inside her hands, peeling apart like the petals of a vast orange desert lily.

"Go," she growled. "Find another way. I'll hold them back."

In two steps, I'd shrugged off the mortal man and dissolved into darkness. Human pains and exhaustion evaporated. The weight of my human body fell away, freeing the truth of me. As Shu's fire filled the tomb's hallways, I funneled power into every chamber and annex and around each column, filling out all the unknown places, stretching far and wide and deep, searching for a way out. And there, a shaft tunneled through the earth, narrow and steep, climbing up through rock to an opening high above the valley. I withdrew each branch I'd cast outward and was almost back beside Shu when a sharp jab of alien power hooked in and yanked me short. I hadn't been expecting it—few things can touch me when I'm made of shadow and hunger—so when the grip snagged, I froze, stunned. For one terrible pause, between a single second and the next, power crawled over me and through me, turning me inside out, over and over. I recoiled and tried to pull free and hide myself in a human body, but the grip didn't budge. Worse, it didn't even appear to notice my struggle. The hold was... *monumental.*

Too much power! The presence filled the tomb and valley and stretched halfway to Luxor. Its power smothered me, crushed in close and pulled me apart all at once. And then, it was gone. Not withdrawn, simply vanished.

I collapsed into my human body, feeling unbalanced and exposed, as though someone had turned my soul inside out, leaving me open, but Shu was alight with flame, and the scorpions sizzled and popped as they came closer and closer. There was no time to chase down the power or consider what it meant.

"Follow me!" I called to Shu, stumbling over my heavy human feet before I could properly get a grip on my body. We ran down corridors and steps and hurried around columned chambers until the small depression in the ceiling revealed itself as a shaft.

"Go!" I shoved Shu ahead.

She dove into the small opening and scurried out of sight.

But I wasn't alone.

The crunching, gnawing, grinding sound of scorpion bodies endlessly tumbling filled the room. Turning, I flung out a hand, "*Hurzd*!" The spellword gripped the scorpions washing up the walls, but their slippery souls wriggled and squirmed, eager to be free. "*Cukkomd*!" I had them, but not for long. It had to be long enough; I didn't have much more power to give.

I scrambled into the shaft after Shu, pushing through pinched rocks and crumbling choke points, until Shu's hand appeared ahead. I flung my hand into hers. She pulled me out into the cool Egyptian night, clapped her hands together, and uttered, *"Dea aeuir kumk uk bescrak!"* Loosely translated to "Die, you sons of bitches."

The ground rumbled, and a blast of rock and dust spewed from the shaft, collapsing our escape route and sealing the scorpions inside.

I fell to my knees, lucky to be upright, and stared at Luxor's city lights twinkling on the sleepy surface of the Nile a few miles away. That had been close, even for me.

We didn't get the skull, but we did escape the tomb mostly alive.

"You get stung?" I asked.

"No."

The power... the hold... Something had gripped me as easily as I flung spellwords around. Weakened and disjointed, I didn't want to stick around and think too hard on it.

"You okay?" Shu asked. I must have looked bad for her to pretend to care. "What happened?" She stood over me, covered in dirt, hair tangled about her face, and clothes torn. Suspicion burned in those purple eyes. I shouldn't have been this weak, shouldn't have been on my knees, grasping at the tattered remnants of my magic.

That kind of power... If Shu got hold of it, or it got hold of her... She already wanted the jars. The temptation would be too great.

"Nothing happened." I wobbled to my feet and spied our Jeep down in the valley. "Let's get back to the hotel."

And away from whatever's back there, I silently added. Isis had a lot to answer for.

CHAPTER 6

It wasn't difficult to find Isis's room. The godstruck hotel staff guarding the door stood out like a neon sign.

"You cannot pass," the guard blocking the door declared, the words at odds with his modern hotel uniform.

I eyed the little guy. He probably weighed half as much as me and looked like one solid punch would drop him for the count. Still, godstruck people didn't reason like everyone else. He'd probably fight me to the death—his death, if Isis ordered it.

I sighed. I didn't want to hurt this guy, but he was in the way of my getting answers. "Just tell her I'm here."

"You cannot pass."

I worked my mouth around the things I wanted to say but knew were useless. "Do I look like I want to be here?" I had half the desert stuck on my torn clothes, the rest I'd swallowed, and I was sure the grinding, gritty parts down my pants were bits of scorpion. "Turn around, open the door, and go tell her Ace is here. Don't make this into a fight, because I'll win."

Two more glassy-eyed hotel staff rounded the corner and squared up to me.

"Isis!" I bellowed. She didn't care if I had to mow down her people to get to her, but I did. "Don't make me call Osiris!"

The guard's left eye twitched as the goddess crawled around inside his head. "You may enter." He stepped aside and opened the double doors.

If my room was luxurious, then her suite was the Taj Mahal. I'd been in smaller museums. Glass, gold, and stone glittered and shone. Different levels broke up the vast open living area while a wall of windows opened onto a balcony that afforded a stunning view of the illuminated Karnak temple less than a mile away. Unfortunately, Her Highness wasn't in sight, meaning I had to wait.

I loitered in the living area for all of five minutes until I decided I was done waiting around for Isis to deem me worthy of her time. She'd buried me and Shu in a tomb after sending us looking for some cursed skull, and I'd almost had my soul violated by something I did *not* want to think about. The bitch goddess would answer my questions NOW.

I found her in the bathroom. Though "bathroom" was too small a word for the bathing temple I'd stumbled into. Thankfully, my feet stopped at the open door, and the rest of me froze there. I'd forgotten I wasn't immune to her, and the sight that greeted me reminded me why I shouldn't be alone with the Goddess of Light. The baths were ridiculously wide and deep. They had to be to accommodate the two women and one guy in the water with her. Isis had her back to me, but she knew I'd arrived. One of the women devotedly braided a small portion of Isis's long black hair, and the other lathered soap over the goddess's bronze shoulders. I couldn't see much of the man from where I stood—just his head as he kissed the goddess's neck and his hands kneading her shoulders. His eyes flicked up to me, glassy and unfocused. He was halfway to being godstruck.

It could have been worse. Osiris could have been here. At least Isis couldn't compel me like her husband, though she did have her own means of manipulation.

I considered coming back with Shukra, but if I left, Isis would know this performance had gotten under my skin.

Nothing about this mattered.

Nothing here meant anything.

Goddess of Light. Do. Not. Touch.

Soul Eater. Godkiller. Ace Dante. I had a job to do, and the bitch had buried me in a tomb. She was not getting to me.

I sauntered over to the sunken bath and tossed a scorpion carcass into the bubbles. Isis's male attendant screamed in a note I didn't think men were capable of and launched himself from the bath so fast that he slipped and collapsed in a spectacular mass of flailing limbs. The two women hadn't seen what I'd thrown into the water, but they did when it bobbed to the surface, its curled black legs half hidden in bubbles and petals. One loosed a blood-curdling scream and scrambled back, while the other froze. Water and bubbles sloshed over the side of the bath, lapping at my sand-caked shoes.

I pinched my lips together, clasped my hands behind my back, and wished Shu were here to see the carnage one dead scorpion could inspire.

Through the theatrics, Isis waited, stone-still. When the screams and whimpers had died down, she reached out a bubble-covered hand and plucked the scorpion carcass out of the water, eying it as though intrigued.

"They come from *mu moka*. I'm immune." *Mostly*, I silently added.

"Of course you are." Isis tossed the damp, dead scorpion toward the whimpering man. He scuttled away, hand clutching his chest. If he thought a dead scorpion was terrifying, he didn't understand the god whose shoulders he'd been massaging.

Isis clicked her fingers. "Leave."

Her attendants collected some of their wits, climbed from the bath, and hurried out of the room, leaving bubbles, flower petals, and pools of water on the tiles.

Submerged up to her shoulders, Isis closed her eyes, the bubbles hiding most of her. I'd seen too much of her too many times, but only with Osiris in the room. Now that we were alone, I wished we weren't.

None of this matters.

Soul Eater. Godkiller. She's the Goddess of Light.

I crouched and dangled my arms over my knees, depositing plenty of sand and dirt all over her shiny floor. "You owe me a hat."

Her gaze cut to me and fury burned in those fiery eyes. "Your presence offends me."

My smile crawled into the corner of my mouth. "Oh, does it? How terrible for Your Highness." She could pretend all she liked, but she'd had plenty of time to throw on a gown if she hadn't wanted me to see her in the flesh. All it took was a click of her fingers. "Why did you bury me and Shu in that tomb?"

She glared ahead, determined not to meet my eyes. A delicate muscle fluttered in her perfect cheek. "The dig team was returning, and you had yet to retrieve the skull. You needed more time."

Water sloshed around her upper arms, plastering her long hair to her skin. I dragged my wandering gaze upward and waited for her to ask about the skull. The seconds ticked on. Water dripped from the ornate tap. Oh, she wanted to ask, but she didn't want me knowing how important this was to her. Never mind her dragging me halfway around the world for this anonymous skull.

"It was Senenmut's tomb," I said, breaking the silence.

Dark lashes flickered once, twice, three times. She already knew whose tomb it was.

"A minor noble," she repeated from the flight over, but I wasn't sure whether it was meant for me or to reinforce something in her mind.

Lies. "Hatshepsut's lover."

Her pert lips tightened. She was excellent at hiding her feelings, but not when I stared at her, unblinking, from two feet away. What was Isis's interest in Hatshepsut and her lover, and why was the missing skull so important that she'd enlisted me to find it and not her husband? The skull was precious to her, for sure. Maybe something I could leverage against her to get out of the godly trap she'd maneuvered me into?

I dipped my filthy fingers in her bathwater. Dirt flaked off and dissolved, clouding her pristine water.

As though my touch had triggered her into motion, Isis rose from the bath and ascended the steps. No man could resist her, and though I wasn't technically human, I was Ace Dante, and I watched her with hungry eyes. A symphony of water and light fell over her naked skin and spilled down curves both soft and hard. The kind of curves I needed to touch.

She didn't bother with a gown and came straight for me, naked as the day the goddess Nut had created her from the stars. I stood and stared her down, because I—gods-be-damned—couldn't *back* down, not now. She'd brought me here. She'd framed me as the Godkiller. She'd made me into her villain. Her beauty couldn't touch me. I couldn't let it.

"The skull wasn't there?" she asked, stopping an inch too close, her dark eyes level with mine.

"No." My heart pounded too heavy in my chest, heating my blood.

Her hardened glare cracked, her lashes lowered, and she looked away.

Do. Not. Touch.

Her pulse beat in her neck, as delicate as butterfly wings.

Don't do it.

Bubbles trailed down her collarbone, gathering at the swell of her breast.

Don't.

She lifted her eyes. So perfect. So bright and clean and light.

Off limits.

Osiris's wife. The Goddess of the Sky, of Light, of Love.

She wants this. If I touch her, she'll have another weapon to wield against me.

The tip of her tongue swept across her bottom lip. "Monster."

I'd touched her in my dreams, tasted her too. I'd risen to the level of a god and worshipped her with my mouth. I wanted her, all men did, but I *wanted* her because of what—of who I was. The monster. The liar, the thief, the devil, the soul eater, the god killer. The part of me that hadn't left the underworld, the part older than my memories could account for, the deeper, darker thing I became, the creature that had gorged on the souls of the innocent... It was so hungry for the light.

I laid my hand on her bare arm, kidding myself that I intended to hold her back. Dust and sand on my fingers turned to mud and smeared across her smooth skin.

"It is no surprise... one such as you..." She whispered the

words too close to my lips, close enough to capture and swallow—to devour. "...desires one such as I."

A loud cough from behind jolted me back. I freed Isis's arm and took one—two hurried steps back, almost tripping over my feet.

"Ace Dante," Shukra pronounced, making sure I heard the weight in her voice.

I swung a glance back at the demon sorceress. She stood rigid inside the bathroom door, arms folded, one eyebrow arched high, her blood-red lips skewed in a less-than-impressed sneer.

"Leave, sorceress," Isis hissed, yanking my attention back to her. A dirty handprint marked her bare arm—a testimony to how close I'd gotten and how close she'd *allowed* me to get. Any closer and Osiris would've had grounds to separate my balls from my body.

"Oh, I will," Shukra replied, "when I've gotten the Soul Eater back."

Fear clamped an icy cage around my hot, racing heart. *Too close.* I turned and brushed by Shukra, briefly resting a grateful hand on her shoulder as I passed.

"You cannot avoid the inevitable, *Mokarakk Oma*." Isis's laughter trailed after me, plucking on the remaining strings of desire. *Too close.*

Shukra's snarl shut off the goddess, and the suite door slammed shut on the rest.

Shukra didn't speak. She walked with me to my room and guarded the door while I threw myself into a bitterly cold shower, washing off the dirt and dregs of poisonous desire for a goddess who'd get me killed.

❧

I GRABBED A TOURIST MAP FROM THE DISPLAY IN THE HOTEL

foyer, then settled in one of the comfortable chairs near the entrance and spread the map open over a low table. Tourists came and went and chatter filled the large open space. That was exactly what I needed after my encounter with Isis: people and normalcy to ground me in being Ace Dante.

The map displayed all the ancient sites around Luxor. An aerial view of the Valley of the Queens and Valley of the Kings was printed on the back. The sites were situated on opposite sides of a solid limestone peak known as *al-Qurn,* which happened to resemble a pyramid. The original valley architects, the leaflet said, had planned to link the two valleys. Finding the rock too treacherous to dig through, they'd abandoned their plans, and today, the valleys remained unconnected. But I knew that history, especially Egyptian history, lied. The skull, the tomb, and the attempt to erase Senenmut from life and death hinted at something more. And Shu and I hadn't been alone in that tomb. Whatever had grabbed me like a toy it could toss around was down there, hidden between the valleys. What if digging *hadn't* stopped? What if another tomb was buried between the valleys?

I'd bet my paycheck—small as it was—that the skull had been a diversion, and Isis was after whatever was buried between the valleys.

Shukra dumped a tumbler of vodka on the table in front of me and slumped into the chair beside mine. She sipped some kind of elaborate multicolored monstrosity of a drink through a straw. Legs crossed, she bounced her sandal, waiting for the explanation that wasn't coming.

I probably should've apologized, or thanked her, but doing either meant I had to admit I was an ass who didn't have the situation with Isis under control.

"Do we need to have the talk?" she asked.

Vodka in hand, I leaned back. "Nothing happened."

Her foot stopped its bouncing. "You forget, I've swallowed your lies for centuries."

I winced and waved her off, repeating, for emphasis, "Nothing happened."

"Denial is a river in Egypt."

"Ha. Ha."

"If you keep telling yourself nothing happened, maybe it'll come true."

The vodka tasted crisp and clean and it went all the way down and warmed my cold soul. "This thing..." I began. Shu raised her brow. "...with Isis."

"There's a thing?"

"She's trying to maneuver me—"

"I noticed."

I leaned forward and lowered the volume of our conversation way down. "I can't come at her head-on. I won't win. I need to come at her from another angle, one she won't see."

"Uh-huh. From behind?" Laughter glittered in her eyes.

I didn't dignify that comment with a reply. "She believes she knows how to get to me. She doesn't."

"Ace..." Shu leaned in, mirroring my posture. "She's the Goddess of Light. No other goddess comes close to what she's capable of. If she wanted to, she'd snuff you out"—she clicked her fingers—"like that. You think Osiris would care? Oh, boohoo, his wife took away his favorite toy. He'll find another schmuck to dance for him. Normally, I wouldn't care, but we all know what happens to me if you get dead. So, do everyone a favor and keep it in your pants, or I will cut it off."

She could try. "If Isis could kill me, she would have centuries ago. The prophecy, her plot to kill Osiris—she needs me to pin the blame on." Then there was the mystery of Isis's note and knowing *what I am*. Shu didn't need to know about that.

"She doesn't *want* to kill you. Remember what happened

to Thoth? All they did was talk, and Osiris wanted the God of Law dead. What I interrupted last night? What do you think Ozzy will do if he found out you had your hands all over his naked wife?"

"He won't find out."

Shukra shook her head, fell back into her chair, and looked around at the people coming and going. "There are worse things than death."

Her words held a wistful tone, the same tone as when she'd said that time didn't change everything. She *had* changed. Not so long ago, figuring out what was going on in her head would have been easier. These days, she was complicated, as was our relationship.

She was right. But I had it under control. "Did you call Cujo?"

"Yeah. There aren't any leads on Mafdet or the burglary at her store and no sign of Cat," she said, intently scanning the tourists, probably for weak spots. Her foot was bouncing again, and she tapped her fingernails on the arm of the chair. "This place... there's old magic here, both close and far away. It's making my skin itch."

I'd been feeling the same since we'd touched down in Egypt. "Luxor stands where the great city of *Waset* once stood."

Shu stopped her fidgeting. I wasn't sure about her true age, but she knew of *Waset*—the city where gods and people had roamed freely, a paradise until the river ran red with blood and the people and buildings turned to sand.

I winced at the memory of buildings toppling, or an image, or whatever it was I'd seen during my unscheduled trip through the Twelve Gates. A world sundered, its people destroyed, Waset's forty-thousand souls... I thought I'd seen New York fall, but what I'd witnessed in the Gates bit at my mind like shards of glass. Those memories didn't want to be remembered, and I wasn't dragging them to the surface without a damn good reason. I already knew I wouldn't like what lurked there.

I picked up my vodka and downed it in one gulp. "How do you feel about scaring the wits out of a few archaeologists?"

Shu's eyes lit up at the prospect of wanton violence. "Do I get to keep any souvenirs?"

CHAPTER 7

The dig team had erected a tent over the tomb's collapsed entrance. Workers passed buckets of rocks down a human line and dumped the debris in a pile farther from the tourist path.

By the time Shu and I arrived, long shadows hung over the site. The heat of the day lingered in the rocks, but the air was free of dust, swept clean by a fresh Nile breeze. I imagined I smelled the spices and flowers from the fields and heard children playing near the water's edge. *Watch for crocodiles*, I'd tell them, steering the beasts away with a look.

Shu clapped me on the back. "Stop daydreaming, Acehole."

She strode toward the tent, pushed inside, and announced in fluent Arabic her name and status with the Ministry of Antiquities. Raised voices drowned out the rest, but Shu's whip-crack reply demanded to see their paperwork, *immediately*. While she kept the archaeology students busy, I drifted around the dig site, trying to blend in.

"May I help you?"

I turned toward the source of the stiff English accent and

squinted against the sun behind the man's broad shoulders. Sweat stained his white shirt a dour gray beneath his arms. A big guy, capable of throwing his weight around, but the voice was prim and proper. London private school, I figured, from an era when politicians and nobles bunked together.

"Senenmut," I said.

"Excuse me?"

"Your tomb. It's Senenmut's."

"Well, that's an interesting theory, Mister..."

I held out my hand. "Dante. Ace Dante."

He gave a little chortle and took my hand in his, nearly taking it off at the wrist. "American! You'd have to be with a name like that."

I laughed along, secretly wondering if he'd find the name *Mokarakk Oma* as hilarious. He stepped out of the sun's glare and looked at me side-on, puzzling out how I'd so confidently guessed what he'd probably spent months trying to prove. His features were naturally bunched together, giving his face a pinched look, but the glee in his small, bright eyes loosened what would otherwise have been a dour expression.

"Doctor Wheeler." A young woman bumbled up to us, swiping a stray lock of dark hair out of her face and smearing sand across her russet-brown cheek. "I'm sorry to interrupt, Doctor. I—" She noticed me and stumbled over her feet and her words. "There's a... someone here. From the Ministry of Antiquities. She wants papers. Our license is all up to date, but she's rather... insistent."

She side-eyed me the way she might watch a scorpion.

Wheeler chortled again. "Oh, a minor misunderstanding, I'm sure. Won't you excuse me, Mister Dante? I just have to..." He was already stalking off, surprisingly agile despite the rocks.

Since he hadn't told me to get off his dig site, I tagged

along and ducked inside the tent where Shukra was barking orders at the interns.

"I'm sorry, you are...?" Wheeler asked Shu, his smile instantly diffusing the tension in the tent.

"Shukra Afroudakis," Shu announced, using one of her many aliases and just a touch of sorceress's suggestive push to endear her to the locals. She looked about as Greek as I looked Irish, but nobody was about to argue with her while she sounded the part. "Ministry of Antiquities." Shu gave him a smile that could melt iron and offered him her hand.

Wheeler took the dainty hand capable of tearing human hearts from chests and brought it to his lips. "I'm charmed, Miss Afroudakis."

"Missis," Shu corrected, disturbingly coy.

"And what a crime that is. I assure you, Missis Afroudakis, all our papers are in order. We're on a legitimate expedition, funded by UCL London. If you would perhaps call your minister, I'm sure we could have this all sorted in a jiffy."

Shu plucked her hand free. "Well, as much as I would love to let you continue working here, I do need to see some identification."

"Of course, of course..." Wheeler waved at the woman who'd alerted him to Shu's presence, and she hurried off to retrieve the relevant documents, I assumed.

"What happened here?" Shu asked, gesturing at the clogged hole in the ground.

"Oh, dreadful thing. The entrance chamber gave way sometime last night. Digging it out again will add several days to our schedule, but we'll get by." Wheeler slicked his fingers through his thinning hair. "Lucky, I suppose, that nobody was inside."

I slipped out of the tent and let Shukra work. She'd have him singing soon enough. I had another target in mind. The young woman whose gaze had lingered on me returned minutes later with various files stacked in her arms. One slipped as she wobbled over the rocks. I caught it before the documents could tumble into the dirt.

"Allow me." I took a few files off the top and helped her deliver them inside the tent. Back outside, she lingered on a small rocky outcropping overlooking the winding path. She braced one hand on her hip, and the other tugged her hair-band free. Her curiously straight dark hair fanned around her shoulders. I'd thought her hair black, but now I saw how the red-tinged valley light summoned an auburn warmth to the dark tones. She had the look of Egypt in her reddish-brown skin, but the accent was sharp English, like Wheeler's.

"Nice view." I stopped beside her and caught her frown out of the corner of my eye. "The valley," I added before the comment had time to sink too deep.

"It is. There's a life to it, you know. It looks desolate from here, but you have to look a little closer to find Egypt's heart." Her words took on a different meaning once her coyness had her breaking eye contact. "There's so much love to be found in the crafting of these tombs... The years they took to make, the craftsmanship. Generations went into this valley. We only see a fraction of what was here before..." She started as though remembering she wasn't alone and laughed dismissively. "I'm just going to stop talking."

"Don't." Her last comment stemmed from self-doubt, which seemed like a crime considering she was right about everything she'd seen and said so far.

She eyed me straight on, questions ticking over in her mind. "I saw you talking with Doctor Wheeler."

"We were discussing Senenmut."

"You were?" She blinked, and tried to hide her surprise before I noticed. "Oh, I didn't think... Never mind."

"The tomb's origins are confidential," I guessed, "but you could say I have an... in."

Curiosity whittled away her suspicions. "Well, I... Doctor Wheeler thought it best not to make the name public. We don't have any proof yet. There are signs, of course. Radar alone tells us the tomb is vast. We know it was constructed for someone important—an official, perhaps a high-born noble—and we know the occupant is—was male."

"You do?" I asked, thinking it wouldn't take much effort to get her to reveal what else they'd discovered.

She smiled softly. "I'm sorry, I don't know your name?"

There was nothing apologetic about her. Fresh-faced and hungry for challenges, she couldn't be more than twenty, but she was willing to look me in the eye despite her instincts warning her off. I offered her my hand. "Ace Dante."

She took my hand, her grip firm and touch soft, and let go too soon. "Like the Inferno?"

"Something like that."

"I'm Masika." She tucked both hands into her linen pants pockets.

The conversation faded, leaving a curious awkwardness that I had no intention of alleviating.

"We're pretty sure it's Senenmut," she blurted and turned to me in a rush of excitement. "I know I shouldn't say, but I can't remember the last big discovery in the valley. Senenmut was... Well, he built much of Hatshepsut's temple and more, like the great obelisks at Karnak. You must have seen those." She reached out as though to grab at the ideas. "He was a powerful man in his time and blessed by the gods. And the people loved him as one of their own—"

"Blessed by which gods exactly?"

She chuckled like the idea was insane, but her laugh faded when all she got from me was a closed smile. "There's a relief in the tomb, probably buried now that the ceiling's gone... Just as you go in the door, it depicts the winged Isis protecting the occupant of the tomb. It was added later, painted over what was already there. It's difficult to decipher, many of the hieroglyphs are missing or scrubbed out, but it appears that Senenmut constructed something vast for the gods. Whatever it was, all references to it were erased." Masika's blue eyes sparkled at the prospect. "If we can prove it's his tomb, that we've finally found him—"

Shukra emerged from the tent, her steps quicker than I'd have liked. Time to leave.

"Can I buy you a drink, Masika? After work tonight?" I started backing up.

"Oh, I... I don't know. No offense, but I don't know you, and we finish late."

She didn't seem like the impulsive type, but she loved her work. That was my angle. "You can tell me more about the Senenmut findings." I turned and strode down the path. "I'm at the Luxor Hotel. Meet me in the reception area at ten."

She'd come; her curiosity ensured it.

❧

SHU HAD GRUMBLED ABOUT THE LACK OF ACTUAL *SCARING the wits* out of the archaeologists. I told her to wait while I tried something subtler than her usual spell-slinger approach. Naturally, that went down about as well as my forbidding her to steal canopic jars. She'd stalked off, telling me she was visiting the night souks—probably to scrounge for spell ingredients.

Before the pair of us could show Doc Wheeler and his students how real ancient Egyptian myths were, I wanted to know more about Isis's connection to Senenmut, and Masika happily obliged me by turning up, as expected, right at ten. She'd dressed down in a long skirt and flowing black blouse with a smattering of decorative sequins along the seams. Her outfit screamed "strictly business," but that curiosity still burned in her eyes. I was a long way from a prize catch, but I could smolder like a professional.

We ambled through the narrow streets of the souk, the crowd ferrying us along. Vendors shouted their wares, trinkets, and clothing. Splashes of color hung out of windows and draped from house to house above us. The rich earthy smells of herbs and incense laced in the air. Masika weathered it like a local, even stopping to haggle down what had started as a ridiculously high-priced scarf. She talked about her work and little else. Occasionally, she attempted to steer the conversation back on me, but with a few nudges, we were back talking about the valleys and her time with Wheeler.

The hour was late, or early, when we stopped outside Karnak. The largest and most recognizable section of the temple glowed in the dark, the light from below setting its stone walls ablaze. Four thousand years of history hummed melodically beneath the oldest parts, now mostly piles of dust and rocks. A shadow of its former glory, the temple still captured the essence of the past, and that alone sent shivers racing beneath my skin.

A pair of armed guards stood at the entrance gates, cigarette tips burning red in the dark. They spotted us and barked for us to move on.

"To think, these buildings have been here for millennia. They've seen so much..." Masika was saying, trailing along behind me. She ran her hand along the crumbling exterior stone wall, needing to touch.

I steered us around the side of Karnak's sprawling complex, heading toward the tiny Temple of Ptah, and found the crumbled section of wall I'd used two nights ago to gain access to the temple grounds.

"I don't think that's a good idea," Masika said, watching me grab a few protruding rocks and start the climb up.

Perched atop the wall, I reached down, inviting her to take my hand. "You only live once."

She knew she shouldn't—that it went against all her fastidious training—but she also really, really wanted to see the hidden parts of Karnak. Parts not open to the public. I smiled, tacking on a wicked glint, and helped her up.

"This is so illegal," she muttered once we'd dropped into the yard inside the complex outside Ptah's little shrine building. Dusting off her skirt, she paused to look around her. Awe shone in her eyes, and her feet carried her forward.

"But so worth it," I added quietly. *"Rarru..."* I whispered.

The temple didn't answer.

A relaxed, slumbering power, like the kind that welcomed me home, tugged on my senses as I trailed after Masika. I let it tickle and tease, careful to keep my magic packed tightly away.

"Tell me about Isis and Senenmut," I urged. We'd talked about legends and rumors, even mentioned a few gods throughout the evening, but this was the first time I'd mentioned Isis.

Masika wandered, hands out, desperate to touch the decorated columns, but she held back. "I don't know much more... Only that it's said Senenmut had the favor of both the goddess and the female pharaoh Hatshepsut. Some believe he was Hatshepsut's lover, but there's no proof of that besides crude ancient graffiti found in the workers' village. The Egyptians were more open to female rulers than we are today, but she still had to depict herself as a man. She was a fierce, proud woman."

"I know."

"Oh, you do?" Masika's smile tilted. She nudged me playfully in the arm. "Do you ever wonder what other treasures are out here, waiting to be discovered?"

"I try not to."

She chuckled, but her curiosity was back, burning like a hungry spark in her eyes. "Where did you say you work?"

I hadn't, and I was saved from answering as we passed through the narrow gulley between the instantly recognizable first pylon and out into the processional way. Over forty ram-headed sphinxes flanked our arrival. They hadn't always lined this west entrance, and more were hidden inside a nearby village, but I wasn't supposed to know what esteemed experts hadn't yet figured out.

Distracted, Masika wandered among the sphinxes. I sauntered a few steps behind, watching her soak up the past and her life's work. She adored the country and its ancient history. It was obvious in the way she spoke and couldn't help revealing all the things she'd discovered during the dig. I'd been right; Wheeler had plucked her out of obscurity from among a Cairo hotel's staff, gotten her a student visa, and tutored her for the last few years in London.

"What if I told you the gods are real and alive today?" I asked, her delight for the old world so infectious I couldn't help but tease.

Masika laughed. "I'd ask you where they were."

Osiris is the mayor of New York, and Isis is probably having her back and other parts massaged by peons in the Luxor Hotel. "For argument's sake, let's say they lost most of their power and the years stole what remained of their sanity."

She laughed again and didn't notice how Karnak greedily ate up the bright sound.

I chuckled along. "Stay with me here. There was a war. The two sides exhausted themselves destroying the land over which they fought." I spread my arms, using the ruined Karnak temple as evidence. "Some of the gods went into hiding, burying themselves from time, while some decided to hide in plain sight, taking on human roles so they might one day rise again."

Masika touched a sphinx's rump. "All right. I'll bite. But it must be difficult to hide a true god, knowing what they once were."

You have no idea. "They were never the most stable of individuals to begin with... Now, let's pretend the gods who didn't bury themselves are getting restless. It's been a long time. Some are bored, some are waiting for whatever the next big upset will be, and some are... orchestrating it." Isis, for one. I knew Osiris also had *plans*. He'd told me as much, but I just didn't know what for... yet.

She cocked her head. "It makes an odd sort of sense, I suppose. We're still discovering tombs. There's no doubt much of Egypt's past is still buried, but where's the evidence these gods truly exist?"

Hidden by me, mostly. I patted her sphinx's nose. "Archaeologists see the science, but they don't or *can't* see the magic."

"Magic?" I waited for the laugh, but it didn't come. "I feel it." She shifted sideways and looked up at me. This close, the temple lights lent her dark skin a soft, golden glow. "How can I not? This place... There's something here. Like you said, I can't explain it, but I know it's close."

"Sleeping." *Slumbering, like the oldest gods.*

"Yes!" She clicked her fingers. The crack echoed through Karnak. "Just because I worship science, it doesn't mean I don't believe in magic, you know."

The night was hot, the air heavy, and as much as I didn't like archaeologists poking around the bones of my past, Masika was different, and this *not-a-date* was drifting into dangerous territory.

I leaned a shoulder against the sphinx's broad neck—it wouldn't mind—and shifted away from Masika before she got the wrong idea. "Now that we're assuming the gods are real and Isis blessed Senenmut for building something that was hidden or destroyed, what do you, in your professional opinion, think that *something* might be?"

"Whatever it is, it was enough to infuriate someone. In antiquity, Senenmut's sarcophagus was moved, *hidden*, and his name was erased..." Masika turned her head, absently admiring Karnak's first pylon behind me, her acute mind skimming over everything she knew. "He disappeared without explanation, according to what we've found. Hatshepsut must have been devastated. I don't think either of them deserved it..." Her gaze roamed my face, and whatever she saw there snagged her attention and her eyes widened. "The light... Your eyes..."

I blinked, shucking off the power that had crept over me, and smiled. "Just the light."

"No, I...." Her dusty fingers touched my cheek. "Who are you... really?"

"A better question is"—Isis's perfectly clear voice sailed through the night like a spear—"*what* is he?" Her smile had all the subtlety of a scythe. She stood in the center of the processional way, wrapped in a deep burgundy cloak clasped shut by a large Eye of Horus buckle.

I shoved Masika behind me, ignoring her yelp. "Isis..."

"Well, isn't this exceedingly sweet? The Soul Eater making friends with local vultures."

This wouldn't end well. I didn't need to hear the slippery malice in Isis's voice to recognize the threat in the leisurely way she moved, knowing she had all the time in the world. She would draw this out and make it hurt in any way she wanted.

"Step out, dear. Let me get a look at you."

I pushed back, pinning Masika against the sphinx. I hated the way she gasped, but Isis would do worse. "Don't," I warned the goddess, with no weight behind my words to back up my threat. Isis couldn't compel me to kill Masika, like her husband would have, but Isis was Isis. All she had to do was lock stares with the girl and Masika would crumble.

"I just want to see," Isis said, her voice dripping sarcasm. "I won't hurt your little bird."

If I didn't let Masika go, Isis would force her out. If I did let her go, she'd walk straight into the arms of an insane goddess. I should've known Isis was watching me. What else did she have to do? I should've gotten the answers from Masika without screwing around. But the temple, this place... I'd just wanted some time with someone who almost understood the old ways, even if she believed it was all fantasy.

"Release her." The compulsion shuddered down my back and shucked off.

I'd stopped Anubis in Duat. I wasn't as powerful here, but Karnak held power I could tap into, if I could wake it. But so could Isis.

"You are making it worse," Isis warned, impatiently sashaying one way then the other like a snake.

Masika's breathing had quickened. Fear, perhaps, or more likely the effect of having Isis's full attention on her. Whatever I did, I had to be fast before Isis's poison got inside Masika's mind.

"Ace?" Masika's hand slipped around my arm. "Who is she? Is that...?"

Everything you think you know but don't. I couldn't tell her. She could still walk away and chalk this up to a weird night in Luxor. She didn't have to get hurt, didn't have to die. *More than darkness.* I wasn't strong enough to fight Isis, but I had other ways to beat her.

"Let her leave," I said, voice hard, "and you can have me."

Isis's brow arched. "*Have you?* Why would I want a creature such as you?" She idly switched direction to wander along the line of sphinxes, trailing a hand over their ram noses and hooked horns. Magic dripped from her fingers in fat, golden globules.

"That's the question we all want answered," I said.

Isis chuckled, and beneath us, the old temple foundation stirred at the sound of the goddess's laughter.

"I am reminded of another time, of you guarding another little bird just like this one. Eyes... like yours..."

I had no idea what she was referring to, but as long as her attention was on me and not Masika, the girl might get out of this alive.

Isis tilted her head. "Mm... how fascinating... I see those moments were taken from you."

"Let her go and you can have me for the rest of the night."

Her liquid laughter flowed like her magic, weaving through temple columns, pouring over cracked rock, and seeping down into the earth. "How you have changed, Soul Eater, and yet not changed at all."

Masika's quick breaths warmed the back of my neck. She had a bright future ahead of her, one I wouldn't allow Isis to steal. "You need me here, and it's not for that skull. So forget the girl, and let's you and me get down to business."

"Do not presume to tell me what to do."

"You wanted me trapped inside that tomb. Why?"

"You're a lie, Soul Eater." Isis lifted her arm and let her hand fall open. "*Girl. Come to me.*"

Masika pushed against my back.

No, no, I couldn't let this happen... Not again. Too many innocent deaths. *More than darkness.* I had the power to stop this.

Masika threw her weight behind a punch, but her weight wasn't much. Her fist bounced off my shoulder. I whirled around and captured her in my arms, but it was useless. Her nails clawed at my face. She'd fight me to get to Isis until I had to hurt her.

Another way...

I spied the sphinx behind her. Magic hummed its siren song through the air. I let Masika go, and she stumbled forward, arms outstretched toward Isis like a little girl desperate to fall into her mother's arms. Isis would break her neck.

I planted a hand on the sphinx's shoulder. "*Cukkomd.*"

Power trilled, spilling in from the temple grounds. It funneled through my flesh and bones, down my arm, infusing the stone. The sphinx's massive ram head creaked. Stones chipped and fell away. A massive lion paw shifted, then the other. Its body rose from its pedestal. It gave its stone head a shake and jumped down, landing with impossible grace. I had its control in my grasp and Karnak's vast reservoir stirring beneath my will. The beast was mine.

"*Vrusacs.*" *Protect.*

The sphinx bounded forward, veering around Masika, and leaped for Isis.

Isis flung up a hand. The sphinx froze in midair.

"Ruv dora aeui!" Isis yelled, spearing me with her gaze.

All the sphinxes trembled awake, moving, creaking, crumbling from their bases.

Okay, so all I'd achieved was pissing Isis off. I could work with that.

"*Run*!" I grabbed Masika's arm and turned on my heel, ignoring her meek cries. A few steps was all it took for Masika to regain control. She ran alongside me, back through the towering columns toward Ptah's temple, where we'd climbed over the wall. "*Go.*"

"What—what's going on?"

I clasped Masika's face in my hands and added a weighty compulsion to my words. *"Run home. Lock the doors. Stay there until morning. Nothing happened here. It was a dream."*

She frowned, but the words were already diving inside her

mind, digging around her thoughts and realigning her memories.

"I'm sorry," I whispered, hoping she didn't remember anything about me or Karnak. "*Go.*"

She climbed over the wall and disappeared over the lip, safely out of sight.

A sphinx slammed into me, knocking me aside as it tried to scramble up the wall after her. Blocks crumbled and the wall groaned.

"No, you don't..." I grabbed its leg and swung it around, tossing it into two more oncoming beasts. All three shattered in a hail of dust. Three more took their places and thundered toward me. Somewhere nearby, Isis seethed. Her power filled the grounds, pushed in, down, around.

I threw out my hands and shook off the illusion of being human. *"Rarru, Kormod. Woda omd rakakbar. Rakakbar ka." Hello, Karnak. Wake and remember. Remember me.*

Isis's laugh danced in the air through the halls and chambers, and the temple lights exploded, plunging us into a starlit darkness.

CHAPTER 8

"Silly *monster*." Isis clicked her tongue against the roof of her mouth, calling all the sphinxes back to her side.

I'd made it as far as the columned Great Hall. There was no point in hiding or running. We were way beyond that. Karnak's great pillars and walls breathed and shuddered, its ancient soul stirring, but Isis was here. What little hold I had over the temple at the beginning, the goddess had taken. Now the temple responded to her, as it should.

I stood, feeling strangely at home among the massive pillars, wrapped in the trappings of history. Perhaps my run-in with Anubis had given me the confidence to square up to a goddess, but it probably had more to do with the fact that, since returning from Duat, with the Rekka under my control and justice on my side, I'd felt different. Stronger. More centered. I'd felt like I was close to finding something that would make me whole. And here, that feeling of rightness solidified.

Thoth had also said something had been taken from me. I felt it too. Felt it in the Gates, in the thousands of souls I'd commanded in Duat, in the seconds I'd compelled the great God Anubis. And I felt it now as I stared Isis down.

If she was going to kill me, expediting my soul to Anubis, I could think of no better place to say goodbye to the world.

Sorry, Shu, but it had to happen eventually.

Isis stopped several strides away. The goddess studied me with a mixture of appalled fascination and disgust. Her sphinxes settled on their haunches, looking again like stone statues, but they were primed to charge if I attacked.

"My husband will not be pleased to learn how you attacked me."

That was a poor card to play and a sign of how unsettled she was. We both knew Osiris would never hear of this.

"Do you really believe I care what Osiris thinks?"

She lifted her chin. Ambient moonlight sharpened her cheekbones, chiseling her features into harder angles. "The jackals tore into your wretched mother with abandon. She barely lifted a claw to stop them. I was there. You were so blinded by rage you didn't notice me. I watched you devour their souls." She drifted closer, moving lightly on her feet. "Your mother's too." Closer still. "Greedy thing, you are," she whispered. "*Soul Eater*."

Icy rage spilled through my veins, but I locked it there. My fingers twitched, dislodging ash from their tips. She had killed Ammit. I'd known it, but to hear her say the words... Another solid piece of me shifted into place.

A thread of golden light outlined her cloak, carving her out of the dark. Gold accents glinted in her skin and shimmered in her eyes. "I find myself inexplicably fascinated by the thing you are, though your very existence should repel me."

She could crush me, but she hadn't. She wouldn't. I *did* have power here, power over her, but I didn't understand why. "What's the skull, really?"

Isis stepped closer. Her fingers unbuckled the Eye of Horus belt, and her cloak fell open, revealing the golden sheen of her skin beneath a gown no thicker than butterfly wings.

"You know what it is," she purred. "You know all the answers."

If only I did. "A key...?"

She tapped a finger against her chin and peered coyly through her lashes. "Clever monster."

"What did you have Senenmut build?"

"Have you ever loved, monster? Are you capable?" She started circling again, inching closer with every step, her steps designed to close me inside her trap. "Perhaps in this body, you believe you can?"

I wasn't about to let her steer the path of my questions. "Whatever you built, you need the skull, the key. You didn't expect it to be missing. Somebody got to Senenmut first despite your efforts to conceal where he was buried." All guesses, but they hit the mark.

She paused, standing close. Her golden brilliance shimmered. "I did not attempt to erase his name. Osiris..." Her lips pinched together. "You once told me there are many kinds of love. You are right." Her hand gently settled on my arm. Instinct screamed at me to pull away, to *get* away, but I bit down on the fear and glared back at her. "Do you look upon my light as monstrous?"

I caught her wrist and twisted it, surprised to find her arm so small in my grip, her bones so fragile. A gasp slipped from her lips, but she didn't struggle.

"What are you so afraid of?" I yanked her close, slipped my free hand around her waist, and spread my fingers against her lower back, soaking up the tantalizing power she radiated.

A fierce resistance burned in her eyes, but something else did too—something like sorrow? But that couldn't be.

"You can stop me." I had her, the Goddess of Light, captured against me. "Stop me." A part of me was desperate for her to push away and end this before it went any further. But instead of pushing, she leaned in and pressed her lithe and deceptively human body against my chest and leg. Magic hummed. Her small body was nothing more than a vessel for the kind of power few got to witness, and even fewer got to hold.

"What am I to you?" I whispered, afraid of the answer more than I was of her.

She brushed her knuckles down my cheek. "You are the Dark."

Goddess of Light.

Do. Not. Touch.

DO-NOT-FUCKING-TOU—

She tasted nothing like I'd imagined in my dreams and like everything the old me, the real me, ached for. I'd always been a creature of hunger, always taken what I shouldn't have, always defied the laws and rules, the gods and their ways. I swam in the River of Souls. I played with demons under the Halls of Judgment. I gorged on the souls of any I could get away with. Devil, liar, thief. And now I was kissing the forbidden, tasting her lips as though they were made of sweet poison, and cupping her face like I might break her. And then the Goddess of Light let me in, swept her tongue over mine, and ground her body against me. It was everything I'd dreamed and more...

A ferocious wave of power slammed over me, driving me to my knees at her feet. The hold I had on my human form wobbled, blurring the world's edges, turning flesh to ash, ash to dust, dust to smoke. I grappled with control, with too much power and too much light. So much light, like I'd swallowed a million souls and wasn't sure whether I could vomit them all back up again or hoard them close. Embers fizzled in the air as I clutched at the dirt like it could save me from breaking apart.

Isis sank her hand into my hair and yanked my head back, sending a blissful dart of pain down my spine. Pain was good. Pain meant I was real.

"What if the apocalypse is not an event?" she hissed, the sorrow burned from her glare and replaced by a rage only a goddess could muster. "What if it's a man?" She flung me down into the dirt. "Find me the skull, monster."

On my side, I watched her stride away—cloak billowing and stars falling around her—and clung to my humanity, afraid her light had almost ripped away whatever made me Ace Dante.

CHAPTER 9

"What by Sekhmet happened to you?" Shu whipped the bed sheet off, exposing my bare ass and my sword, Alysdair, lying next to me. "We were supposed to meet two hours ago to frighten Wheeler and his baby archaeologists back to England."

Eyes closed, I buried my face in the pillow. *"Ba suma,"* I mumbled. *Be gone.*

Shu snorted at my use of the old language. "You have three seconds to get out of bed before I turn it into nails."

I waved a hand, indicating for her to go away or go ahead, I wasn't sure which. My head was stuffed with cotton and my body felt like half of Karnak was lying on top of me. The come down from whatever Isis had hit me with wasn't going anywhere anytime soon, and neither was I.

"Three."

"Go, do whatever you have to," I grumbled.

"Two." Shu's unique blend of manipulated power hummed around the room like a sirocco wind.

I turned my head and cracked an eye open. "Nails?"

She blinked. Her dark eyebrows plunged into a scowl, and then she lunged, hands outstretched. I had Alysdair up, the blade pressed against her throat before she could put into motion whatever she had planned. The sword sang, hungry for Shukra's damned soul.

Concern had her gaze stuttering. She wet her lips and pushed her fingers against the blade, easing it back. "Cool your jets, Acehole." Her words were the usual lighthearted dig, but the humor sounded strained.

She hadn't physically attacked me in decades, but that didn't mean she wouldn't. But this was Shu... The new Shu... She was... different? My heart pounded hot and heavy. Old instincts crawled out of the box I'd hidden them in. Twisted, dark souls should be destroyed. That's what I did. Soul Eater. But... time had passed. Things had changed.

I let her push the sword away from her throat only because she was powering down. "Step back," I ordered.

She lifted her hands and took several deliberate steps back.

I could see the questions in her eyes, but I wasn't playing games, and neither was she. A few ancient words, a single strike, and Alysdair might take a bite. The sword couldn't devour her—Osiris had seen to that when he cursed us together—but it could cripple her power for weeks.

"I thought we were past all this..." Her lips twisted around something sour.

I swung my legs over the edge of the bed and rested Alysdair beside me. Yes, we were beyond all this. Maybe I'd overreacted, or maybe I'd stopped her from laying a spell on me while I wasn't in my right mind. Now that I was upright, the hotel room dipped and swayed, fuzzy at the edges. I pinched the bridge of my nose and shook my head to realign my thoughts.

"I gave up fucking redemption for you," she growled, "you

ungrateful lizard. If I was going to hurt you, I wouldn't let you see me coming, and you'd only damn well know about it afterward. How much did you drink last night?"

She was right. What the hell was wrong with me?

Shu dug into her jacket pocket and plucked out my cell. She showed it to me, making sure I knew it wasn't a grenade, and tossed it onto the bed. It landed screen side up.

Missed calls: 6

From: Osiris.

Monster, Isis's sweet voice whispered in my ear. Memories from a few hours ago. I swallowed what felt like glass in my throat and dragged a hand down my face. Ozzy was calling me. That was bad. He'd probably realized his wife had disappeared and wanted his pet Soul Eater to find her.

"Thought you'd like to know," Shu offered.

I rubbed my finger and thumb over my mouth and scratched at the whiskers along my jaw, debating how much to tell Shu. Nothing, probably. Stick to business. The tomb, the archaeologists. Focus on that. She'd gone to see the archaeologists without me? "You went to the dig site anyway?" I asked, sounding as though I'd been dragged up from the depths of the earth and over hot stones.

"Empty."

"What?"

She shrugged. "Nobody showed up for work today. It's probably a religious holiday or something."

Isis had them. Of course she did. All my magical flexing had done was expose a weakness, and now she'd use those people—including Masika—as leverage. Gods be damned, I should have scared the information out of them like Shukra had suggested.

I growled out a noise that may not have been entirely human and pushed to my feet. I had clothes around here somewhere... "We have to find the skull." I found my pants and shirt forming a trail from the door to the bed. I had no memory of leaving Karnak or returning to the hotel. That was also bad. Me and missing memories never end well. "Are there any reports of anything... unusual last night?"

"Anything unusual like?" Shu glowered, familiar with where this was going.

"Missing people besides the archaeologists?" I winced, remembering all too well what I'd done to the witches. But Alysdair had been cursed ... and I couldn't be cursed, and Thoth was gone. Alysdair wasn't cursed now, and I hadn't carried my sword on me last night. Just Isis. She'd been on me, around me, in me... What had happened? There was Karnak, and... a kiss that had felt like a thunderbolt.

"The hotel staff was chattering about something this morning. The sphinxes lining Karnak's entrance have all moved."

The sphinxes, Karnak, Isis, power... all that power. The hotel room tilted, almost spilling me onto the floor. If it hadn't been for the sideboard, I'd have gone down. Shu made a move like she was considering helping me. By Sekhmet, what had Isis done to me?

The mirror above the sideboard revealed a reflection that didn't look like mine.

"That's what I was going to tell you... before you lost your shit..." Shu's voice trailed off. She was probably still speaking, but my thudding heart drowned her out. *More than darkness. You are the Dark. Monster. Nameless One.* My eyes were golden, just like Osiris's. I blinked, and they stayed golden. I blinked again and willed the power away. Still they stayed golden, flecked with slivers of black. This sometimes happened in Duat. If they didn't go black from swallowing too many souls, they brightened. But not here, never here, and never for long. Another blink. I glared at my face, a snarl quivering on my lips.

"Sudk ba dokmad," Gods be damned.

"What happened?" Shu whispered, the note of fear strange in her voice.

I swallowed and squeezed my eyes closed to hide from the truth. "Nothing. Nothing happened." But it was a lie. And like the ruins of the old world, all the lies that had shored me up through the centuries had begun to crumble.

❧

THE PLATEAU OUTSIDE HATSHEPSUT'S TEMPLE WAS HOTTER than hell, and I should know, seeing as hell was a new name for an old place that happened to be my backyard.

Three lax security guards waved Shu and me through broken security scanners without looking up from their card game, sparing themselves my wrath, which had been building since I'd left the hotel. In fact, probably long before then, since Isis had cornered me in Macy's and demanded I go to Egypt.

"C'mon," I grunted at Shu and started the long march up the first of three long slopes. The pair of sunglasses I'd paid too much for in the souk threw a shadow over the temple's three plateaus. The once great mortuary temple now resembled the carcass of a long-dead animal, its ribs picked clean by sand, sun, and the ravages of time.

Shukra kept in step with me, ready to smack me down should I start raining ash and embers. She was right to be on guard. I had a track record for losing control, but I wouldn't slip, not here.

"This place used to be beautiful," I muttered, more to myself than Shu.

I reached the first terrace and squinted back into the sun. Gardens had once painted the grounds in lush greens. Flowers had splashed color as far as the eye could see, and the woody, spiced smell of frankincense had filled the air. Now all I saw was sand, and all I could smell was baked rock. A dead land for a dead pharaoh and a dead world.

"It still is," she replied.

"This is not beauty."

My cell chirped in my pocket. I ignored it and headed through the terrace toward the second ramp. The heat had driven all but the most foolish of visitors away, and recent terrorist attacks had spooked off the rest. Besides one or two ambling guards, Shu and I had the temple to ourselves. That made what I was about to do a little easier.

"Ace—"

I knew what she was about to say. Osiris. The calls. "What do you want from me? If I answer, he'll tell me to find Isis. If I refuse, he'll compel me."

"So? You know where she is."

"And Osiris won't find it suspicious that I happen to be here, in Egypt, *with his wife?*"

"Should he?"

I marched on, rocks and gravel crunching under my shoes. Shu stuck to me like my shadow.

"You were at Karnak last night, with Isis. You woke Karnak and got high on power. I don't need to be a genius to figure that out. I can smell the temple and the bitch goddess all over you. Not to mention the eyes—"

"Shu, get off my back."

"I will when you stop acting like a kid caught with his fingers in a god's—"

I whirled on her and ripped the shades off. "Do not push me, Shukra. We came here for the skull. *That* is all that matters."

"Why?!" she snapped back. The question bounced around the empty temple until the limestone soaked it up. "Why are we even doing this? Why don't you tell Osiris exactly what's happening?"

"Do you want to see what your insides look like decorating his bedroom wall?"

She ground her teeth. "What happened in the tomb when we were running from the scorpions, and don't tell me *nothing happened.* I know you, and this is you being an ass because you're scared. So, for once in your self-centered life, let me in so I can help. You don't have to do this alone."

Let her in? The condemned demon sorceress who would have, at one time, sold a million innocent souls to see me strung up? But she wasn't that creature anymore. She had changed, and so had I.

Tell her, or don't tell her? Trust her, or don't trust her? A sudden realization dumped icy water over me. She'd given up redemption to save my ass from Anubis. I needed her on this with me. I needed her to keep me straight, to keep me from myself. *I needed Shukra.* Sekhmet's ass, when had that happened?

"The skull is a key," I admitted, trusting she wouldn't add to my growing list of problems by going after it herself.

"Go on." She didn't seem surprised, but very little surprised her.

I had to start trusting her, and there wouldn't be a "good" disaster to test on her. "There's something hidden between the burial valleys," I began, watching her closely. "It got to me in the tomb, just a nudge, but it's powerful. Isis needs that skull to get to it. Last night, she followed me to Karnak and threatened the archaeologist I was trying to get answers from. And now the whole team is gone. It's no mystery who has them."

"And?"

"So we get the skull first and get Isis to release the archaeologists. If we have to, we destroy the skull before any god can get their claws on it and whatever it unlocks."

"Okay." She waited, expecting more.

"That's it. I've got nothing else."

"*Is* that it? Because all that seems like something Ace Dante can handle, but you aren't handling it."

Was this really the place to discuss the dreams, the things I'd seen in the Twelve Gates, how being back in Egypt was shaving away my hard-earned armor, and how Isis seemed to know exactly how to push my buttons? "There's something about Isis..." I turned away from Shu and scanned the jagged cliffs where they dipped toward the Nile valley. "She brings out the worst in me." And I couldn't say more, not here. Back in New York, where the air bites and the rain smells like asphalt, I'd tell Shu everything, but not here in the land that listened.

"Look at my face." She used a finger to circle her face. A smile played on her pink lips—the same mildly amused one that always rested there whether she was watching kittens play on YouTube or skinning snakes alive. Her dark eyes regarded me with a level coolness unique to Shukra. The look said, *"I've seen it all, done it all, and your drama is so cute, but seriously."* "Do I look like Anubis?" she asked.

"What?"

"I'm not judging you. Isis gets in everybody's head. It's her MO. When you're ready to tell me what's really going on, I'll be here. Until then, let's go get this skull and save some stupid archaeologists." She headed off toward the third and final terrace, calling back, "It's up here, right?"

I watched a heat haze ripple over her as she strode up the ramp. Exactly when had Shukra and I become friends instead of enemies? Something had shifted long before she gave up redemption in the Halls of Judgment, and I hadn't seen it—or hadn't wanted to see it.

Amun Ra's sanctuary was a small chamber dug out of the rock face in the deepest part of Hatshepsut's temple. Among Egypt's sprawling temples, vast pyramids, and monumental sphinxes, this nook inside Hatshepsut's mortuary didn't stand out. Few people knew the sanctuary's true purpose.

"Djeser-Djeseru," Holy of holies. I drifted deeper into the shadows, toward the waiting statue of Amun Ra. A thick rope barred the way to stop tourists from getting too close. A lick of cool air ran around the back of my neck, and a sense of space swelled around me, making this tiny room suddenly seem cavernous. My eyes were human. I couldn't *see* the truth, but I didn't need to.

"Rarru..." I closed my eyes and breathed in, drawing superheated dusty air over my tongue. The temple and its power didn't stir. I hadn't expected it to, but it was polite to say hello.

"Maybe you're firing duds," Shu remarked from behind me.

A smile tugged on my lips. I kept my eyes closed and my mind level.

"All these spaces to nowhere and enough pillars to hold up Osiris's ego... Makes you wonder what they were all compensating for. In humans, I hear large buildings compensate for small genitals. You'd know all about that..."

I let her prattle on, hopped over the rope, and dropped to my knees in front of Amun Ra's statue. During the winter solstice, a shaft of sunlight pierced the gloom and illuminated Ra. Then it traveled to where a similar statue of Osiris had once sat. Its spot was empty, the statue stolen or destroyed long ago. Few outside of Duat knew the true reason for that spike of light. Today wasn't the winter solstice, but I'd never been one to follow rules. Brute magical force should serve just as well.

"Ace?"

"Stay back." I rolled up my sleeves. "Give me a minute." And pressed my hands to the warm stone floor. I spread my fingers wide and puffed out a breath, blowing the dust away.

"The guards..."

"A minute, Shu..." I mumbled, bowing forward, low enough to kiss the sand. *C'mon, Djeser-Djeseru. Welcome an old friend. "Ovam kur ka, kur I ok uk sra oer, sra aorsr, sra resrs, omd sra dord. Ovam, omd varcuka ka srruisr."* The words fell from my lips, like thoughts breathed to life. These were the same words I'd used to open a doorway to Duat, but without water and in this temple, they took on a different meaning. To rouse, to tempt.

Shu's smooth, melodic voice scratched at my concentration. I pushed the outside aside and buried deep into my waiting power, as hungry and wild as always, and more so since my return from Duat, since walking again in the forgotten land. The truth of me twitched to life and sank into the stone, seeping through the tiny cracks and fissures, seeking what lay beyond.

"Ovam kur ka." Open for me.

And there, buried deep inside the cliffs behind the statue, the slumbering power stirred, stretching awake. Stone shuddered, dust rained from above, and with a yawning groan, Amun Ra's sanctuary shifted. The walls clunked from mystical mechanisms grinding into motion. When I looked up, the sanctuary's back wall split in two and opened inward, revealing a colorfully decorated passage untouched by time. It glittered and sang with magic and life, bright and playful.

Spluttered Arabic spoiled the moment. "*Waquf. Tawaqqaf hunak*!" a male voice barked.

The two guards stared at the temple's new extension with awe-widened eyes. Shukra stood beside them, wearing a similar expression. What had I been saying about nothing surprising her? "Er, Shu?"

She blinked, realized we had company, snatched the rifle from the first guard, and cracked the butt under his jaw. He sprawled across the floor, out cold. The second guard spent too long fumbling for his gun—seeing an ancient temple *move* and burst to life in an explosion of color would dull anyone's reflexes. Shu stamped on his boot, smacked the flat of the rifle's stock against his cheek, and then drove it into his gut. She floored him with a punch that made me wince. He fell to the ground and stayed there.

"Shu?! You were meant to distract them, not beat them unconscious."

She threw the gun down and strode toward the passage opening, the guards forgotten. "That"—she pointed —"shouldn't be there." She jabbed a finger at the opening, eyeing it side-on for tricks and traps.

"Technically, it's not *there*." We didn't have all day to sight-see. I shoved her into the passage and followed close behind. "Have I surprised the unsurprisable?"

The doors rumbled closed behind us. I pressed a hand to the wall. "*Rarru...*"

"*Raku*," a distant whisper replied. *Home*. "See, not exactly Egypt... This is part of Duat. A back door..."

Painted hieroglyphs glowed, illuminating several hundred meters of passage to an opening that hinted at something glittering gold beyond. The air again smelled like frankincense, not the arid desert. Distant memories sailed toward me on the familiar breeze, but I barred them access. I didn't have time to indulge the past. We needed information, and this was how we'd get it.

Shu grumbled something about too much color blinding her eyes and said scornfully, "*You* shouldn't have the power to wake this place, whatever or wherever it is..."

"I shouldn't have a lot of things," I agreed, losing my smile.

Shu glanced over her shoulder, more questions burning in her eyes. And doubts too. She saw her Soul Eater, the man she'd been cursed to for several centuries, but she wondered if she recognized me. Shukra was no fool. The unspoken questions simmered between us.

"You've been here before?" she asked.

"No."

She didn't believe me, and as we reached the end of the passage, her questions were forgotten.

I hadn't been sure what we'd find inside, but now that we were here, some of my memories slotted neatly into place. The walls were plastered with scrolls. Shelves overflowed with unmarked papyrus, others with half-finished works. Endless piles of scrolls stretched into the distance. I'd seen a fragment of this place when Shukra had helped me search my memories for the source of the witch-killing curse.

"What is this place?"

"Thoth's library. A sanctuary of truth." As I spoke, a mound of scrolls shifted. Some toppled from the pile and clattered to the decorated floor, spilling open. The massive pile heaved, and a huge spotted cat emerged from inside. She stretched her massive paws. Her back dipped and her tail flicked high. Five times the size of a leopard, she yawned, stretching her man-eating jaws wide, and growled low. But her eyes remained closed, as they had since Thoth had blinded her.

She sniffed the air. *"I smell old souls and sin."* She purred the words and somehow worked her feline lips around them. "*Mokarakk Oma*."

"Who's that?" Shu whispered.

I didn't have time to reply. The cat sprang, claws extended, jaws open wide.

Shu and I lunged apart. A plinth brought my leap to an abrupt end and almost dislocated my shoulder. Something priceless shattered around me. Buckling around the impact, I twisted in time to see the cat land gracefully on all fours and turn toward me. Hunched low, she prowled forward.

"Aeui kruird mus ba rara, Sudderrar." You should not be here, Godkiller.

I was beginning to agree.

CHAPTER 10

"E*coka kur sra Senen-mut kcrurrk." I came for the Senenmut scrolls.*

If I've learned anything in my years as Osiris's dog, it's that whatever I do, the gods always win. Knowing that, I could pretty much ask whatever I wanted, because the outcome would always be the same.

"You wake me for this?" the cat grumbled, fat paws plodding forward. "Why would I give *you* anything?"

I was used to dealing with big cats. Bast, my ex-wife, was one in her spare time, but even she wasn't as large as this goddess, Sesha. Sesha was mythical-beast large.

Shukra's power shivered through the air, and Sesha's closed-eyes narrowed in response. The goddess would tear into Shu, might even kill her, and then I'd have to go back to Duat and find her soul before Anubis did. There was a chance Osiris might find her first, and then we'd all be suffering. I could probably stop Sesha, or at least distract her, but the last thing I wanted was to throw-down here and make yet another godly enemy. Good thing I knew of another way to distract a goddess of the feline persuasion.

Catching Shu's eye, I shook my head, and the unsettling itch of her power fell away, but she watched, armed with a spell on her lips.

"You've slept for a long time," I said, keeping my tone conversational. Slowly, I planted both hands on the floor and pushed to my feet, careful not to make any sudden movements. I was the prey here. "Wouldn't you like to play a game?"

"A game?" She shook her head and flicked one furred, triangular ear, then sat on her rump and snuffled the air. "What games does the Nameless One play?"

"Answer me this: what turns everything around but does not move?"

Shukra pulled a *what-the-hell* face, demonstrating exactly why I dealt with the gods and she stayed away from them.

Sesha's laugh rumbled through her belly. She pushed onto her feet and ambled around me, panting and tasting the air. "A mirror. Try harder, little river beast."

Sesha was famed for her love of riddles.

"I'll play some more"—I rolled my shoulder, working out the ache to distract myself from my rattling nerves—"if you give me Senenmut's scrolls."

"I do not think I will give you anything, *Mokarakk Oma*, but I will keep you here if Ammit allows. We could play for a long time. Would you like that, little crocodile?"

I lifted a hand, making sure I had Shu's attention, pointed deeper into the rest of the library, and then pressed a finger to my lips. She moved away, deathly silent.

Sesha didn't know Ammit was dead. She also probably didn't know I was cursed to Osiris. She'd been locked in the library ever since Thoth had caught her snooping and gouged out her eyes as punishment. Sesha was from the old world. I wondered if she even knew of the sundering and how the world had changed beyond her recognition. Probably not. Ignorance was bliss.

"Do you ever think about freedom, Sesha?" I asked.

"Ask me your riddles, *Mokarakk Oma,* and return to Duat." She lifted a fat paw and licked at the pads.

I eyed Shu as she scanned the shelves of scrolls. "Until I am measured, I am not known. How you miss me when I have flown. What am I?"

Sesha was in motion again, her speckled coat smooth over powerful muscles. She brushed up against some shelves in a very catlike chin rub. "Mm..." she purred.

A quick glance revealed Shu still searching, but the library was vast. The chance of her finding the correct scrolls was slim.

I started my own slow exploration as Sesha prowled around columns. Senenmut's architect scrolls were human-made, not god-made. They'd be frayed and imperfect. If I could get close enough, I should be able to tell the difference. I just needed a rough idea where they could be.

"Time," Sesha answered, adding a yowl. She pounced in front of me, bringing my wanderings up short. "Another, prey. Tell me another." Her canine teeth glinted, each the size of my forearm.

"The scrolls?"

"Another!" she demanded, but her ear flicked and her tail twitched, all toward a section of aged scrolls piled high.

"Very well..." I drifted forward, scanning the stacks of rolled papyrus. She couldn't *see* what I was doing, but she'd figure it out if I didn't distract her. "What has four legs in the morning, two legs in the afternoon, and three legs at night?"

Sesha draped herself over a step, scooped up her tail, and licked at its white tip. "Four, two, three..." The tip quivered. She swatted it and playfully chewed.

As she considered the riddle, I spotted a familiar symbol

peeking out from the torn edge of a closed scroll: a jackal with the head of a snake. The same symbol was on Ammit's missing box, and I'd recently carved it into a witch's hand as a clue to snap myself out of Thoth's curse. The symbol had stalked me for over a year, and here it was again, on a scroll in Thoth's library. There was no way I was leaving without it. I flexed my fingers and inched the scroll from beneath the stack. Almost free, a ragged edge snagged on one of its neighbors, and the stack of scrolls clattered to the floor.

"Run!" Shukra yelled. Her power flooded the air, choking out the sweet smells with the oily, burnt-diesel odor of her magic.

I whirled in time to avoid the blur of massive cat. Sesha plowed into the shelves, sending scrolls flying. I managed three strides before a paw the size of a tree trunk hooked a leg out from under me. The floor rushed up to smack me in the chin, and the scroll slipped from my grip and rolled away.

Sesha's thundering bounds approached. I flipped onto my back and got both legs up in time to catch the goddess's pounce and throw her over me. She tumbled over and then released her claws, slicing into stone with an ear-splitting screech.

I dashed forward, snatched up the scroll, and ran toward Shukra. The demon sorceress's eyes glowed an eerie liquid green as she chanted. A pulsing, heaving cloud of hissing things appeared out of nowhere. Locusts. Shu flung them at the goddess.

Sesha's roar rocked the floor.

There—old, damaged scrolls. Battered and stained, torn and frayed, and along their edges, one name stood out: Senenmut. I scooped up an armful, still running.

"Thief!" Sesha howled, spinning around and around as she snapped and swatted at the locusts. "Thoth will hear of this. Thoth will punish you as he did me!"

Shu's spell snapped, and the locusts scattered. We bolted for the passage. Shu ran on, but I stopped at the passageway and spread my arms, touching the walls on either side of me. "Stay here, Sesha. The world is not what it was. Stay here and remember the old times. You'll thank me for it."

The big cat goddess lifted her head and sniffed at the air once more, smelling the new world on my clothes—heat, pollutants, and the metallic taste of technology. She pulled her lips back in a snarl.

"*Cukkomd.*" I poured too much power into the walls and stepped back as fragments of ceiling collapsed around me. The last thing anyone needed was Sesha free in the new world. I'd tell Osiris she was awake. The gods were his problem, not mine.

The passage collapsed on her enraged howl, driving Shu and me out into the stifling hot terrace. Amun Ra's sanctuary doors sealed shut with a thunderous bang, and the library was once again hidden from all.

Shu panted, hands on her thighs. She looked over at the bundle of scrolls under my arm, grinned, and held out her fist.

I bumped my fist with hers and said, "Best tomb raiders in Egypt."

"You know it."

SENENMUT'S SCROLLS WERE SCATTERED LIKE RUGS ACROSS the hotel room's tiled floor. I'd considered taking the scrolls and Shu into Luxor, somewhere away from Isis, but I figured the goddess was less likely to suspect anything if we stayed closer to the hotel. So Shu and I had ordered a room service banquet and charged it to Isis's account before settling down for a long night of reading.

Most of the scrolls had seen better days. Despite the care

of their custodian, the majority were badly damaged, not helped by removing them from Thoth's library. Opened, they spread from the bed to the door, depicting Senenmut's various building projects throughout Waset/Luxor and into the Theban valleys. All the plans corresponded with sites I recognized, all but one...

"There..." I stepped around the scroll, folded my arms, and glared down at the faded outline depicting a *pr-djt,* a flat-topped tomb, the oldest style of burial shrines. They looked like stepped pyramids. "Where is that?"

"Aren't there several mastabas left?" Shu replied, using the Arabic name for that design.

"This one is different. See there, it's tilted, facing down. Most are aligned on an east-west axis, aiding the soul's passage into the underworld, but this one faces the opposite way, as though whoever it was built to contain is barred from the underworld." A tiny cartouche marked the corner, so small I almost missed it. "And there's that..."

Shu poured herself a glass of wine, took a gulp, and maneuvered her way around the scrolls. "Ah..." She'd spotted the name. "*Suddakk uk Resrs.*"

Goddess of Light.

Shu snickered. "That's a small tomb for the bitch queen."

"Because it's not for her, but she commissioned it." Crouching down, I flicked the scroll on an angle, admiring the sharp lines intersecting the tomb from all directions. "Passages," I murmured. But something about the angle of those passages seemed familiar.

I moved around the scrolls, searching for the ancient, faded map of the two valleys. Shuffling a few scrolls around, I got the maps resting against Isis's tomb in the center. "You see it?"

Shu squinted. "The tombs in both valleys line up... They

all have passages running toward this one." She pointed at a vast maze of a tomb. "Whose tomb is that?"

"*That* is the largest tomb in the Valley of the Kings, built for Ramesses the Second's many sons, if you believe recent *experts*. KV Five. It's still being excavated." I knew the tomb only from the news reports of its discovery in the nineties. I'd dismissed it as yet another piece of the old world, dug up, turned over, and exposed to prying eyes.

"After what I've seen today," Shu said, "you're about to tell me it's some kind of elaborate bathing temple for the gods or some other ridiculously self-indulgent nonsense—like where they went to worship cats or something?"

I crossed the room and snatched up my cell, ignoring the missed calls notifications. A quick Wi-Fi search revealed KV5's existing layout as it stood today. I knew what it *wasn't*. "KV Five's not a tomb, despite what the *professionals* think. I reckon it's a grand entrance for whatever Senenmut built Isis. Look at the layout. The passageways are too small to transport sarcophagi through. It was never meant to be used for burials. It doesn't even look like the rest of the tombs in the Valley of the Kings."

I held the phone out to Shu. She took it and turned the phone sideways to glance at the layout.

"Those passages lead right to Isis's secret, deep inside the al-Qurn peak," I continued. "And now we know where the doorway is."

"But no key." Shu sighed.

"But no key," I echoed.

She handed the phone back and downed the rest of her wine like it was water. I took Shu's glass, refilled it from the bottle, and poured a glass of my own, my thoughts wandering. The wine was local, rich and syrupy, the type sold unofficially under the table in the souks or freely given in six-star hotels.

Karnak glowed in the distance, drawing me out onto the

terrace and into the warm early evening. I leaned against the balustrade, glass in hand. "It was thought Senenmut died before Hatshepsut, though his body was never found—until now. Rumor in Duat is that Hatshepsut's nephew had Senenmut killed to weaken his aunt's reign. It worked. Not long after Senenmut's disappearance, Hatshepsut died and her nephew took the throne."

Shu leaned against the balcony wall behind me, keeping to the shadows. "How very *Game of Thrones*."

"If you're a goddess and you have your subjects building a secret tomb, what do you think happens to those subjects once the job is done?"

"Ah."

"Exactly. History made Hatshepsut's nephew a convenient scapegoat. I'd take a stab in the dark and guess Senenmut ran or Isis had him killed. His body survived, but the head... That was removed before he was entombed. We need to find out by who. Clearly, Isis didn't do it. She had no idea the skull wasn't inside."

"Hatshepsut?" Shu suggested and came forward. She leaned on the balustrade and looked down at the almost perfect surface of the pool in the gardens below.

"It seems likely. Or priests, if she had them. Either way, they're all long dead."

"So how do we talk to a few thousand-year-old dead pharaohs?" Shu smiled sympathetically, already knowing the answer. She had her talents—making spells from body parts and generally being a thorn in my side—and I had mine—getting up close and personal with eternal souls.

"It's not that simple. Her soul could've passed over into the afterlife. If it hasn't and it's still around in Duat, it'll be in the River." The last time I set foot in the River, the ferryman's boat had capsized and the souls had tricked me into believing Cat had drowned. I no longer had the promise of redemption hanging over my head, but souls weren't the easiest things to reason with at the best of times. Finding Hatshepsut in the River would be like finding a single grain of sand in the desert... in a sandstorm. "Even if I find the soul and focus it enough to get it talking, there's no guarantee it'll remember anything from the correct past life. And there's the fact I eat souls, so... yah know, there's that hurdle to get over."

"Pussy."

My laugh came out as a snort. "You think I'm afraid to go back after everything that happened?"

"No, I think you're afraid of you. But what the hell do I know? I'm just a rotten soul in a pantsuit."

Until recently, I'd have agreed. "You're more than that."

She waved a hand, sweeping the comment away. "Keep all that gooey friendly shit to yourself."

"I mean it. You're a good friend, and lately, I've been an ass."

"You've been an ass for centuries." She threw her glare to the starlit sky. "Sekhmet save me, the self-centered soul eater had an epiphany." When she was done mocking me, she leaned a hip against the rail and asked, "Since we're BFFs, when will you tell me about the other scroll you stole?"

"What other scroll?" I lied smoothly.

"The one you hid while room service kept me busy."

Oh-kay then. And there I was thinking I'd gotten away with that. I opened my mouth and—

"Bullshit me and this budding new friendship of ours is as dead as your common sense."

—closed it again.

Shu examined her nails, their points liable to turn into claws at any moment.

It *was* time I stop shutting Shu out. She'd earned my

trust. I gestured for her to follow and stepped back inside the hotel room. "Shut the doors."

As the doors clicked closed, I removed the scroll from under the bed—the best hiding place I could find on short notice—and set it down on the sheets. I frowned at it instead of opening it right away. Rolled up, it didn't look like anything special. Just another papyrus, like all the others in Sesha's library.

Shu sighed dramatically, gripped the edge, and yanked it open, revealing a spread of red hieroglyphs. I scanned the text with Shu silent beside me, but the words, and their meaning, might as well have been the ramblings of a madman.

"It doesn't make any sense," I grumbled. I'd hoped it would say something about the mark and why or how it was connected to me.

"Some godstruck priest wrote that a thousand years ago, and you're surprised it's nonsense?" Shu eyed me, not the scroll, but I couldn't tear myself away from the text.

The writing on the scroll was a list of devastations. Floods, crops set ablaze, villages reduced to dust. On and on the list went, with no explanation, just disasters, one after another. Halfway down the scroll, the list cut off.

"It's unfinished." I flipped the scroll, expecting to find more on the back. Nothing besides that one symbol in the bottom right-hand corner, facing inward. The snake-headed jackal. The symbol that kept stalking me. The same damn symbol on Ammit's box, a box warded against me, a box that was missing, along with Mafdet. Osiris knew the symbol, but he'd lied about as soon as I'd brought it up. Why? Why would a god as powerful as Osiris need to lie? Why, why, why...

I snatched up the scroll and headed for the door.

"Ace?"

Isis's room was a few floors above. She'd be inside.

"Why is that scroll so important to you?" Shu followed.

She didn't know about the symbol or the missing box, or how it kept haunting me like I *should* know it. The less she knew, the less it could come back and bite us in the ass.

Isis had answers. The goddess knew exactly what was going on. She would know what the symbol meant, and while I was there, she could tell me exactly where the missing archaeologists were and the real reason she'd brought me to Egypt.

"Ace..." Shu slammed her hand against the wall next to the elevator, her glare true and hard. "If you go up there like this, she'll get her claws into you."

The elevator numbers counted down.

"I can handle Isis." I pushed the words through clenched teeth.

"Oh, you can? Because from where I'm standing, it looks a lot like she can handle you. Just because you got Anubis to sit for you, doesn't mean Isis will. She's screwing with you, making you doubt everything you know, making you think you have power over her. She's setting you up, and you're walking right into it."

Fifteen, fourteen, thirteen... The floor numbers ticked down like time running out. "I do have power over her."

"No, Ace. Only the power she's given you, and she'll take it away."

I met Shu's uncompromising glare. She knew me, probably knew me better than anyone this side of Duat. Cursed together, we had no choice but to know each other. But she understood, too. Like me, she'd been trapped under a god's thumb for centuries. She'd endured their special kind of mental torture. "I'm done being used. Aren't you? She'll tell me what I want to know—"

"Or what?"

"Or I'll call Osiris back and tell him everything that's happening here. Every. Thing. He'll have to listen. He knows it anyway. He knows his wife is a scheming, power-hungry bitch, but he's too afraid of her to do anything."

Ten, nine, eight... I wasn't backing down.

"Ace, look at me."

I did, and I saw the passage of time in the lines around her eyes, and her lips were no longer twisted in a snarl but pressed into a reluctant grimace. There was nothing Shu could say or do to stop me, and that's why she looked sorry.

"There are things you should know," she murmured.

"That's exactly why I need to do this."

"No, you don't understand—"

The elevator pinged, and the door rumbled open. I stepped inside and jabbed the penthouse button.

Shu stuck her foot in the door. "Don't go. Let me finish."

"If I don't go now, then nothing will change. Aren't you tired? Because I am. I am so fucking tired, Shukra. Tired of the gods and their insanity. For too long, Osiris has clicked his fingers, and I've snapped to heel. I am done with it. I'm done with all of it. The gods, the hate, the feeling that everyone knows the secrets but me. And I'm starting with Isis."

"Rile her up and she'll kill you."

"She would have already if she could."

"Memories can be altered. She could have already tried and you wouldn't remember."

"I'd know it," I dismissed.

Shukra bit her lower lip, the gesture entirely too human. "As a friend, I'm asking you not to go."

I smiled, but it was a slippery thing that quickly fell from my lips. "I don't have a choice." This wouldn't end with the skull. Isis would have another task for me, and deeper inside her claws would sink. If I didn't stop her, she'd use me over and over, pitching me against her husband until Osiris figured it out. Better for me to tell him on my terms, whatever the fallout may be. But before then, and before she killed the archaeologists like she had Senenmut to keep her secret tomb safe, I needed Isis's answers.

Shu nodded once and freed the door. "Whatever happens, you know I'll always have your back."

At my stiff nod, the door closed, and the car lifted me toward Isis's floor. I'd confront Isis and demand my answers, whatever it took. The goddess didn't control me. I had control. Soul Eater, Nameless One, Godkiller. She should fear me, and she did. I knew it. I'd seen the fear in her eyes. She knew too much, knew everything. And now she'd tell me why.

The elevator pinged and the door opened. I stepped out into the hallway where I'd met the godstruck hotel staff member barring her door, but now the man who'd refused to let me pass sat slumped against the wall, his guts sliced open. Blood leaked in a vast pool around him. His eyes were wide, dead and unseeing.

Two others lay motionless where they'd fallen. The door to Isis's suite hung open, marked by bloody handprints. The carnage continued inside. A dozen dead, the splatter of blood bright against silk sheets and polished floors. The stench of wet meat coated my tongue and clogged my throat.

For one horrible, gut-wrenching moment, I feared the body-shaped mound on the bed was Isis. If she was dead, Osiris wouldn't stop at killing me; he'd go on slaughtering until half the world was queued up at the Twelve Gates. I tugged back the sheet, saw the dull brown eyes of another woman, and shuddered. Dead, all of them, but not Isis.

These people, Isis's godstruck staff, had been caught unawares and slaughtered before they'd had a chance to run. Something powerful had done this. Isis herself?

The goddess's hijab lay discarded near the window. I lifted it from a pool of blood and breathed in Isis's intoxicating flowery scent. She wasn't careless enough to leave a scene like this behind. It didn't seem possible—Isis was too powerful—but what if she'd been taken?

I wrapped the hijab around my fist and dialed Shu on my cell.

"That was fast," she answered.

"We have a problem."

CHAPTER 11

"We should tell Osiris," Shu said.

I put that gem of advice down to the fact she wasn't thinking clearly while surrounded by so many dead bodies and potential spell ingredients.

Crouching beside the body of a young man, I whispered, "*Daquir*," and the last corpse dissolved into ash. I couldn't devour the blood, but hopefully Isis would see to that when she returned. *If she returns.* She would. She had to. Otherwise, the fallout from Osiris would be biblical. The only upside was, as the messenger, he'd obliterate me first so I wouldn't get to see the reign of wrath he'd herald in across several continents.

"Isis is fine," I said and straightened. "Like you said, nothing can touch the Goddess of Light. The last thing we need is an emotional Osiris breathing down our necks."

Shu paced back and forth by the open terrace doors. Her sandals hissed through the fallen ash from the other bodies I'd disposed of, stirring the remains and lifting the acrid smell into the air.

"So let's get the next plane back to New York and pretend we were never here."

Back and forth, she paced. This wasn't like Shu. Her nervousness couldn't be over the fact that a dozen people had died here, and it certainly wasn't because Isis was missing. But something had her spooked.

"We can't leave. There are innocent people caught in this. The archaeologists—"

"There are more archaeologists," Shu snapped. "I'll find you another one."

"That's not what I meant," I replied carefully, like handling glass. "I can't abandon them."

"Ugh. I preferred you when you didn't think you were some kind of hero."

"I've changed, and so have you. You don't really want to leave those people with Isis?"

"Don't I?" She stopped her pacing and fixed a hand on her cocked hip. "What good is a dead hero?"

I stood and brushed ash from my pants. "We're staying."

The curse made sure she couldn't leave without me, and she wasn't about to throw down over it, even if she was pissed. I moved around the blood splatters, letting her stew in her own anger.

"What if Isis killed them?" she asked.

I regarded the blood splatters and smears staining the floor, couch, bed, and walls. Isis was more than capable of this—she'd set the jackals on Ammit and ordered me to kill via Osiris many times in the past—but what was her angle here? Why would she slaughter people she'd seen as her servants? "Why?"

Shu's laugh cracked like a whip. "How did you even survive childhood? She has a history of setting you up. You walk into a massacre in Isis's suite, with no witnesses, and you don't think she might, oh, I don't know, pin it on you for husband dearest? Let's pretend, for a second, that Osiris knows you're here with Isis. What's Isis going to do? She won't admit she asked you to come here. She'll drop you in the shit and make you out to be the enraged jealous psychopath who stalked her halfway around the world and her as the sweet damsel in distress."

It was plausible. "Enraged jealous psychopath?"

"That's your takeaway from everything I said?"

"Even Osiris isn't stupid enough to see Isis as a damsel in distress."

Shukra's glare had gone from mildly irritated to outright death ray. "You need to take this more seriously. This is my life too."

And there was the truth. She didn't care about any of this, just saving her own hide. Maybe a little of the old Shu still existed in there. "Do you know if Osiris is on his way here?"

"No, I—"

"So quit worrying about something that hasn't happened and worry about the fact that something or someone had the magical balls to break into Isis's suite and kill her people." I brushed ash from my hands and gestured around the room, still in disarray. "Do you sense any fragments of magic?"

Closing her eyes, she shook out her hands and stilled. "There is something under all your ash... It's familiar." She opened her eyes. "The magic, it tastes like the scorpion curse from Senenmut's tomb. Whoever set that trap was here."

That trap had been set when the sarcophagus was sealed thousands of years ago. People didn't live long, so we were dealing with a god. "That narrows it down."

For another god to attack Isis so brazenly, they were either looking to destabilize the existing peace, or they were insane. Or both. Why did it always have to be gods, and why was I always stuck in the middle?

"Do you think we released more than the scorpions when we cracked open that sarcophagus?"

Shu caught my meaning. "We would have known." But she didn't sound sure.

"Let's take another look at that tomb."

❧

STARLIGHT GLITTERED ABOVE THE VALLEY OF THE QUEENS, and a swollen moon poured light over cooling rocks and settling sand.

Shu lurched the Jeep to a halt where tourist buses parked during the day, stirring up clouds of dust. Up ahead, people blocked the valley. Lots and lots of people lined the paths winding between the steep valley sides. Hundreds of figures, at least.

Shu cut the engine. "What the...?"

I gripped the top of the windshield and stood, letting the sight sink in. Silence. The kind of rare, natural silence only found in isolated pockets of the world, or the sound of magic breathing in. Crowds don't do silence. Either those people weren't real, or something else was at work here.

Shu and I wove our way through the silent lines of people. Some were draped in ankle-length *galabiya* robes, while others had arrived straight from their air-conditioned offices. All stared up at the valley, eyes glassy.

Shu waved a hand in front of a man's face and shrugged when he didn't react.

Godstruck, all of them.

We pushed on through, following the eerie trail of their glares to a recently excavated hole in the ground that marked Senenmut's tomb. The debris had been shifted. Deep inside, hieroglyphs glowed and shimmered like living things. The scorpions were long gone, but something *was* down there—

something that had drawn all these people out of their daily routines and called them here.

Shu peered down the ladder. "I'm not climbing into a hole in the ground with an unknown god."

"Pussy."

"I don't *do* gods. That's your specialty." She backed away from the hole and thumbed at the blank-eyed groupies. "I'll keep an eye on these fools."

I grabbed the ladder, wondered if this might be the last hole in the ground I'd climb into that wasn't my grave, and descended.

The tomb could have been finished yesterday. What had been dusty and faded during my last visit now shone with freshly painted brilliance and magic. I reached out a hand, more by reflex than thought, and ancient power pulled me in, just like in Duat.

"*Rarru...*" I whispered.

The power purred in response and brushed up against me, welcoming me home.

I could have lingered for hours, absorbing the old world and its magic, but time wouldn't wait. People had died and more would follow if I didn't get to the bottom of what Isis had stirred up.

But it wasn't a god that we'd missed after triggering the curse. Isis stood in the burial chamber beside Senenmut's sarcophagus, startlingly small for a goddess. With her head bowed, her long straight hair cascaded down her back in a black waterfall. I could have mistaken her for a temple girl if not for the gold shimmering through her thin gown.

"Isis—" I considered reciting her respectful greeting—it seemed fitting—but her words cut me off.

"It was not meant to be this way."

Approaching a goddess from behind was a fine way to find yourself flung against a wall, especially considering the *unusual* circumstances. I hung back, my power tied up good and tight.

Part of me wanted to grab her shoulders and shake all the answers out of her. Whatever crisis she was having, I didn't *want* to care, but I feared part of me did care, and that was worse. What kind of monster cared about the Goddess of Light? She didn't do vulnerable, and yet here she was, broken, and it was screwing with my unyielding hatred for her. Her drama was Osiris's problem, not mine. I had a job to do. Free the archaeologists. Find the skull. Destroy it. Go back to New York. Polish off the bottle of vodka in my bottom drawer. And be the surly asshole everyone loved to hate.

"Someone got inside your hotel room. Your staff were killed." I spoke softly, but in the confines of the burial chamber, my words landed like hammer blows.

Her shoulders tensed. She hadn't known. "You don't understand. No soul understands..."

And I didn't want to understand either. "Isis, someone killed your people—"

"I do not care."

"And there are hundreds of people outside—"

"I do not care about them!" she hissed, but didn't turn. "I do not care about their lives, or yours, or anything in this miserable mockery of a world."

From the cutting edge in her voice, I knew what I'd see on her face the second she looked at me. Fury. It would have been wise to back away slowly and leave. Shu and I could go back to the bar and pretend this had nothing to do with either of us. But I couldn't walk away. Isis had answers and the people outside needed dispersing. That meant figuring out what was wrong with her and talking her down.

I took a single step inside the burial chamber. Stone slammed shut behind me with a ground-trembling clap. That answered my question about whether I could walk away.

Now I was trapped with a goddess I couldn't decide if I wanted to fuck or kill and a headless, desiccated corpse. Great.

"The hardest part of eternal life is caring," she whispered so softly, the words not meant for me. Maybe they were meant for the dead architect or the voices in her head. Who knew? Not me, and that was the problem.

The hardest part of *my* life was avoiding her husband and staying alive, but I kept silent and moved around the foot of the sarcophagus. I could see her face now. Tears had left tracks down her bronze cheeks, but I'd been right. Fury burned fiercely in her finely black-lined eyes.

"Goddess of Light..." I bowed my head. "No mortal man has ever—" Her sudden, smooth laughter interrupted. Insanity clawed at her laughter, threatening to shred it.

"Oh, silly, lying monster. You have no idea of the irony in your words." She looked up, and her smile cracked and remade as she fought to hold on to it. "My dearest husband devised that ridiculous greeting and demanded all must say it to my face. Over and over I must listen to it, century after century, while wearing my smile and pretending each time it does not cut like a blade. After a few millennia of marriage, you may begin to understand what it is truly like."

Understand Osiris and Isis, siblings and lovers? That wouldn't happen. And right now, my patience with her breakdown was wearing thin.

"Isis, your people were killed. Don't you want to—"

Her eyes flashed. "Take that tone with me, *Mokarakk Oma,* and I will rip your tongue out."

Her threat was a warning slash in my direction, nothing more. Whatever she was angry at, it wasn't me—for once.

"Who killed your staff?"

"They do not matter." Her lashes fluttered, and she dropped her gaze to the corpse. "In many ways, I admire her.

She and I were alike once. Women lost in the shadow of men."

Sekhmet grant me the patience to deal with emotional goddesses. "Who, Isis? Help me, and I can help you." *Does Shu feel like this when talking with me?*

"She rose to power, defying centuries of tradition. She begged me for assistance, spent hours in my temple on her knees. And I favored her with my blessing because I saw in her a passion I had so long ago lost."

She was talking about Hatshepsut. A piece of knowledge clicked into place, and the way Isis looked down at Senenmut's body began to make a lot more sense.

Love. Isis had asked me if I was capable of it. I didn't believe she was, not anymore. But she clearly had been. Once.

"*You* loved Senenmut?" I asked, trying not to sound skeptical and failing.

"He was a good man. A fair man. Intelligent and loyal and caring. Good men are a rare thing, monster, and forever is a long time to love." She spread her hand over the top of the sarcophagus, resting it gently over the sculpted wrists crossed over the heart. "But he was mortal, and I... I am not."

I was wrong. She hadn't killed Senenmut to keep her secrets safe. That look in her eyes had nothing to do with anger and everything to do with regret.

She looked up, right at me, an urgency now in her words. "There were rumors, of course. Hatshepsut grew jealous when Senenmut built for me the grandest shrine of all. Not a tomb, but a place I might take my slumber and wait the ages away. He toiled for years in secret, and I loved him for his honor, his pride, and his heart, and for doing what my husband had refused to do. Osiris would not let me sleep. And so I loved a good man, but he could not love me. A mortal cannot love a god as we are blinding, but I loved him,

Mokarakk Oma, and for the first time in centuries, I cared." Her words trembled, as did her lips.

I knew where this tale was going, and it did not have a happy ending. It never does when gods fall in love with mortals.

"He discovered the truth," she whispered.

It didn't take a genius to figure out who "he" was.

"My husband's spies watched and waited. They did not strike. Instead, they would tell my husband of the times Senenmut came to me. You see, like those people outside lining the valley, Senenmut could not help himself. I knew it was a mistake, but for so long, I had been cold and empty. I needed him, just the simple love of a good man, not a god. Do you see, *Mokarakk Oma*? Can you possibly understand?"

"Yes." And I did. I knew what it felt like to be an empty, uncaring creature, and I knew what it felt like to be a man who cared and loved and hated and feared. I knew which I'd rather be.

Spite cut her laugh in half. "A monster like you understands. Osiris was blind. A mortal's love made me happy, but my husband's love could not." Isis's fingers curled into her palm, turning her hand into a fist. "Osiris commanded Hatshepsut's court to string Senenmut up. She loved him too, but she could not compete, and so her love turned to jealousy, and in my husband, she found an ally. They tore Senenmut apart in a spectacle for all to see, drawing out his death for nine days and nights, and then, when it was done and Senenmut's soul had passed on, Osiris destroyed his name so he would be forgotten in this life and the next." A shiver ran through Isis, the memories haunting her. "It was because of my love that a good man died..."

"He wasn't forgotten. His soul was weighed," I said, remembering Ammit's account. It was the least I could offer Isis. "Ammit told me his soul was one of the lightest she'd known. He took his journey through the Twelve Gates and entered the Afterlife."

Her wide eyes glistened. "And I should feel something for that, but I do not care. I cannot care. I was once the Goddess of Light, of Creation, of All Things, of Love. But it has been so long. Time has carved out my heart." She stepped away from the sarcophagus and looked around us. Her expression hardened, and her vulnerabilities vanished behind a mask as golden and lifeless as that of the sarcophagus. She looked at me as though realizing she'd told her inner most secrets to her worst enemy and now needed to either crush me or twist me up in knots so tight I'd have no hope of escaping. "And so it has come to *this*. That it is you here with me."

I was losing her. She'd shut me out and stalk off, and I'd be stuck at the beginning all over again, with no answers and archaeologists to find. "Isis, the skull..."

"Hatshepsut or Osiris moved the skull. All I want is to find it and set right the past." She flicked her hand and the stone door rumbled open. "As we can't ask either, I... I do not know what can be done."

I stretched an arm across the doorway, blocking Isis's exit. "I do." I had to go back to Duat, to the River of Souls, but before then... She'd been about to snarl and flick me out of the way like the insignificant bug she thought I was, but my words pulled her up short. "But you must release Masika, Wheeler, and the other archaeologists."

"The vultures? Why would I have them?"

"You don't?"

"Perhaps they moved on to pick another carcass clean. Now *move from my path*."

Her compulsion trickled off, but I obeyed and stepped aside, then followed her out of the tomb. Shu backed well away from the goddess and joined the ranks of dull-eyed people hanging out in the valley. As Isis passed them, they dropped to their knees and kissed the earth. She ignored every single one.

I trailed behind, watching people fall like dominoes. None of them would remember this, but that didn't make it any less disturbing. If she could control the population of a small village without lifting a finger, what could she do with the power of whatever was hidden in the valley at her disposal?

I had to find that skull and the many answers along with it.

CHAPTER 12

Shu and I had the hotel to ourselves. Whether it was Isis's influence or just off-season, I wasn't sure, but I didn't doubt Isis had her claws in the entire hotel staff. They hurried back and forth, reminding me of the priests who used to manage the temples during the various and many old-world festivals.

Shu was taking advantage of the unmanned hotel bar. She saw me coming and scooped up an unbranded brown bottle and sloshed some of its contents into a glass.

"Do I want to know?" I asked, giving the liquid an experimental swirl.

"Vodka. I think. Or gasoline. They don't appear to really do alcohol in Egypt."

"Technically, it's illegal, but hotels get away with it." I planted myself at the bar and downed the drink in one gulp. Fire lit up my insides, but before I could splutter something obscene, the raging inferno tempered to something mildly survivable. "I'll assume you aren't poisoning me," I wheezed and held out the glass for another.

"I like this." She swept a hand at the stretch of bar top. "I should kick out the diner in my building and open a bar back home. Call it *Shu's Sins*."

Her bar here today was a little on the empty side. "You don't have any customers."

"That's the best bit. Got all these drinks to myself. Can you imagine the concoctions? I'd add some ancient Egyptian spice to the cocktails and see if I can't shake up those uptight city boys and make them *see* magic." She waggled her fingers.

I laughed along with her and made a mental note not to allow Shu to purchase any bar equipment.

"So, tell me all the juicy gossip," she asked, enjoying her role as bartender. "What happened in the tomb?"

"Isis got all teary-eyed over the past. I asked her to release the archaeologists before I go back to Duat, and she denied having them." The thought of revealing everything Isis had said about Senenmut and her affair tightened my insides. My moral compass had broken years ago, sending me off course at about the same time I started consuming innocent souls because they tasted so damn good, but despite my disliking Isis, she'd told me the intimate truth of her affair with Senenmut. Somewhere inside, it felt wrong to spill all that information to Shu. Maybe my moral compass had life left in it.

"That's it?" Shu frowned.

"More or less."

"What's her connection to the dead guy?" She sipped her drink and hissed at its potency.

"They were lovers."

Shu spat her drink out. "Wait, wait... Isis, the wife of the God of Fertility, was screwing around with a human lover? Oh, that's... that's gold. Oh, that's... I like that. The bastard deserves it. Can you imagine Osiris's face when he found out his wife was banging a mortal, not even a noble? She couldn't fuck anything worse—besides you."

There was that moral compass again, nudging me back on

course. I should hate Isis—I did hate Isis—but I also understood some of what she'd endured with her husband forever at her side. I mean, Osiris was all ego, and the "I'm the God of Fertility so I can screw anything" excuse had gotten old real quick. I'd happily take Alysdair and carve him in two if I thought killing him would stick, and I'd only been under his curse for a few centuries. After a few millennia, I'd be out-of-my-tree insane too.

"Cujo's gonna love this," Shu chuckled.

"You can't tell him."

"Why not?"

"Keep him out of it. We've had too many close calls already."

She shrugged. "It's Cujo. He's the only person I can share all my weird shit with besides you, and you *are* my weird shit."

"Shu, this isn't a game. If Osiris or Isis learns there's a mortal who knows as much as he does, they'll kill him." Isis's tale of Senenmut's death was fresh in my mind. If Cujo died over my mistakes, I couldn't bear it. No more deaths. *More than darkness.* "Just don't tell him. You shouldn't even be screwing around with a mortal. It never ends well." I'd screwed around with a few in my time. Loved a few too. I still remembered them and how their souls had tasted as they slipped all the way down.

The next glass of vodka went down smoother.

"That's rich coming from you, golden eyes."

I winced. "Still gold?"

"Yup. If your skin were a shade darker, you'd look a lot like Osiris. It's disturbing."

"It should have worn off by now."

"That's what you get for wallowing in Karnak's magic."

I grunted a non-committal sound that could have been an agreement. Shu and I might be on sharing terms, but I wasn't about to tell her that the power overload had come from Isis's kiss. If I did, Cujo would hear about it, and then I'd have them both on my back.

Drowning my thoughts in vodka had always worked, so I tried the same now.

Shu watched the drinks line up and go down one after another and kept her comments to herself. But her permanently arched eyebrow peaked even higher as she asked, "Do you believe Isis? About her not knowing where the archaeologists are?"

"She has them. Gods are predictable. Right now, I'm playing nice like an obedient little soul eater, but she'll use those people as leverage the second I need a nudge. She can't compel me like her husband can, so she needs another stick to beat me with. She'll tell me where they are eventually. Until then, she'll keep them alive." I tipped my refilled glass. "That's the game the gods play. She can't help herself."

"So the Soul Eater is best of friends with the Goddess of Light, huh?"

I smiled. Here I was talking with my centuries-old enemy over drinks. "Her guard is down, and I have her confidence. I can use that."

Shu picked up a cloth and started scrubbing down the bar top like she'd been manning this bar her whole life. "Just make sure she doesn't burn you."

I smiled into my drink. Shu. Domesticated. I hadn't expected that. "It's sweet."

"What is?" she grumbled.

"How much you care."

"About you?" She snorted. "If we weren't cursed together, I'd steal a bus just to run you down and grind your lifeless carcass into the asphalt."

"Sure you would, Shu." I set my drink down and pushed away from the bar, heading out toward the pool.

"Where's my tip?" she called.

"Don't mix spirits."

"What?"

"I'll be back by dawn."

"You better be, Acehole. What do I do if her Immortal Bitch-Highness comes looking for her pet?"

"She knows where I am..."

A quick dip in the pool and a few ancient words later, I was in Duat—home. Not New York home, but the home that burns human eyes, tries to drown you in curious sprites, and talks back when you say hello. I jogged across the plaza and headed straight for the vast columned portico over the Halls of Judgment, keeping my head up and my strides true. A few curious souls watched me pass. The last time I was home, I'd had my back whipped to shreds and my heart weighed against the Feather of Truth, and I'd pissed off Anubis and trapped the legendary Rekka into my service by way of a slave cuff. My relationship with Duat and its denizens was rocky, so say the least. These were not the best of times. They believed I'd consumed innocent souls (I had), that I'd killed Ammit the Great Devourer (I hadn't), and that Thoth's recent demise was by the tip of my blade (it was). The only place I felt relatively safe was with the ferryman, and only then because nobody dared attack him.

He greeted me with his usual hollow-faced hooded cloak and linen-wrapped fingers. His boat whispered up to the small timber dock and rocked to a gentle stop.

"*Mokarakk Oma, kicr rok cromsad.*" *Nameless One, much has changed.* His voice didn't come from a mouth—as far as I knew, he didn't have one. It trickled into my ear, speaking to more than my physical being, speaking to my soul.

I held out two dimes for passage across the River, but the ferryman didn't move to take them. He'd never refused before. I stilled, knocked off my stride. The ferryman had never refused anyone.

"They're good." I laughed, injecting confidence into the words to hide my fear.

"Kraa vokkosa." Free passage.

I looked at him side-on. Where was the catch? "Take them."

"Much has changed. *You* have changed. Come."

When the ferryman says get in the boat, you get in the damn boat without arguing. The skiff rocked as my weight unsettled it, and then we were silently drifting forward into the fog's cool embrace. But free passage? I'd never heard of such a thing. Even Osiris paid his way.

"There is unrest around your name," the ferryman said.

I stayed quiet and gazed into the dark water, waiting for the faces to float to the surface. In Duat, there was always unrest around my many names.

"The balance is upset. Many ripples, you cause."

None of this was news. "Anubis is going to pin his next drama on me, huh? Let him."

"You are not as you should be and not as you appear to be. *Inpu* seeks answers."

Inpu was Anubis's old name, and the ferryman was using it to remind me whose fur I'd rubbed the wrong way. "He's not the only one." Everyone wanted answers. They could get in line behind me.

The ferryman's shoulders shifted. He turned and maneuvered himself around so he sat in front of me. He was still all cloak and nothing under the hood, but now all that nothingness was aimed at me. My skin itched under the weight of his attention. He rarely faced his passengers, preferring to remain indifferent and aloof.

The boat sailed on without him at the helm, and the quiet clung on.

"Cracks are appearing," he said, his whispered words no

more substantial than the fog touching my face. "Sands are shifting. The souls feel it, as do you."

I'd known it since returning too late to save Ammit from the jackals. I'd been out of practice back then, but with my recent visit and the *things* I'd witnessed in the Gates? Bossing Anubis around, commanding legions of snakes—none of that was normal, or as normal as life in Duat could get.

"You own the Rekka," he added.

And there was that. "That was an accident. I had the slave cuff. I didn't expect it to—"

He lifted his hand, silencing me. "You have never lied to me. Do not start now. You challenged the God of the Damned in the weighing chamber. You command the Rekka. You defy all who seek to strike you down. And you survived the Twelve Gates. All this while you are shackled by Osiris. Do not speak of accidents. I *know* you."

Silenced, I worked my jaw around the denials. It was all a collection of accidents, wasn't it? I hadn't orchestrated any of it. All I was trying to do was survive the gods. Or was there more to it? More I wasn't seeing? "I'm beginning to wonder if anyone knows me, including me."

"When your mother found you as a child in the River, she came to me and asked what you were. I could not answer her."

"I know that." The infamous Nameless One. Ammit's charge. The orphaned upstart.

"You misunderstand. I *could not* answer. Your life, your presence here, it is a wrongness. You do not belong."

Duat had been my home longer than I'd been Ace Dante. And now that was also a lie? "Then where do I belong, ferryman? Tell me, because the gods either won't, can't, or don't know, and I'm tired of looking to them for answers." I searched the swirling black inside his hood, seeking a scrap of tangible presence to latch on to, but all I got was a sense that something slippery and surreal was looking back at me. "If you know something, tell me."

He waited. Water lapped against the boat's hull in time with the steady beat of my heart. If he had answers, now was the time to tell me. Inside, in the old part of me, my instincts squirmed to get away from the ferryman's glare.

"The River gave you up all those years ago because you did not belong. You have changed."

These weren't answers; they were more riddles. The ferryman couldn't help me, but I hadn't expected him to. This trip wasn't about me.

"*Kurrae*," I told him. *Sorry*.

His hood shifted as he realized what I was about to do. He reached out, but it was already too late. I dived over the edge into the water.

The Great River swallowed me down the way it used to, wrapping me up in its cool embrace. I dove deeper and kicked hard, seeking out the dark and ignoring the burn in my lungs. The ferryman could pluck me out at any moment, but I was gambling that he wouldn't. Not yet. He'd always allowed me time in the River as a boy.

Vague faces loomed, curious at first, but when they remembered who—what I was, they dissolved, part of them remembering how to be afraid. Deeper I pushed until the pressure in my chest threatened to tear me open.

Surrounded by darkness and figures made of glistening webs of light, I leveled out and spread my arms. I relaxed the hold on my physical self and let the real me spread outward. All I had to do was let go of being human. My human heart thudded harder, and my human lungs burned. The more I clung to my false life, the more my thoughts swam and my body protested. It had been a long time since I'd swum freely in the River, but I hadn't forgotten. I just needed to remember what I was. I wasn't about to die. That wasn't how this worked. Water slipped through my lips, over my tongue, and down my throat. My body bucked around the invasion, and instincts screamed at me to launch toward the surface. And then, as easily as flicking a switch, the water turned to air, my body into shadow. The pain vanished and the ethereal realm of souls opened. The River had let me in.

"*Hatshepsut...*" I whispered, reaching farther and freeing more of the power I kept contained.

You're not a soul eater, but you're very good at pretending to be.

For a moment, the memory of Cat's voice jarred with this time and place, almost yanking me back into my Ace Dante skin. She'd almost drowned here when the souls tried to take her, but she'd survived. She *was* still alive. Wasn't she? I ignored the doubt, ignored everything I didn't understand, and focused on my task.

"*Hatshepsut...*" I cast the name outward.

Souls drifted in schools, glimmering in the corners of my vision, not wanting me to single them out, but curious enough to drift closer.

I repeated Hatshepsut's name, pushing power into the summons and sending it out into the endless nothing. I wouldn't be able to hunt down the correct soul without spending years in the River, and time was not on my side. My only chance was the soul coming to me.

The truth has been taken from you. Thoth's words, but his soul wasn't here either, just the memory of him inside my head, chipping away at the human parts of me.

"*Mokarakk Oma.*" A glimmer of light separated from the others. It twitched and danced, spinning like a sun catcher. *"I kaa aeui. Yui ora sra Daquirar muv?" "I see you. You are the Great Devourer now?"* Like the ferryman's voice, the soul's grew inside my thoughts.

"I'm not here to further your journey. Do you remember your life as Hatshepsut?"

"Fragments."

"Senenmut, do you remember him?"

"*Yes,*" the voice hissed.

"Osiris had him killed?" I tested, circling my shadows around the light.

"I searched, but Senenmut is not here?"

"No."

"I had hoped..."

"Hatshepsut, Senenmut was killed. We found his body, but his skull was removed before his entombment. Do you remember who removed it?"

"Yes... He created wonderful things for her. He loved me and I him, but she was too much. She took him from me and turned him into a slave. I saved him... but he is not here."

"The skull?" I had to keep the soul focused. If its attention drifted, I might never get it back.

"The skull is a lock or a key or just a skull?"

"Yes, the key. Do you know where it is?"

"My priests took it and sent it far from me, from her. It must never be returned to the body, never combined with night and day."

I was losing it. "Why?"

"The shrine between the valleys is a cage. It must not be opened."

A cage. Not a prison or a tomb, but a cage. Creatures and beasts are caged. It could mean nothing, could just be a poorly chosen word, but I filed it away for later. "Where did they send the skull?"

"Do not open it, Mokarakk Oma." The soul pulsated and spun faster. *"You must not. The cage cracks, even now. I feel it. How can you not?"*

"I want to stop it from being opened—"

"No. This is her doing. You were sent by her!" The soul blazed too brightly, raging against the dark. I'd caught the soul in my hand before I was even aware I'd moved. It jerked and bucked, but my wrappings of shadow and ash entombed it. *I*

could crush it. I wanted to. Crush it, make it mine, feed off its brilliance and all the others here. A river of souls, a river of power. All mine to steal, to take, to consume—

The world and my place in it slid backward at a pace too fast for me to see. I lost my grip on the soul as the waters rushed by, tearing at the threads of my true self until I wrapped them all back up, folding the dark of me into something resembling a human again.

The ferryman unceremoniously dumped me on the dockside. The spooky bastard loomed over me. "You never learn."

On my hands and knees, I spluttered up lungfuls of water. That was good. Being a solid flesh and blood human was definitely good. For a second there, I'd almost forgotten... *"Kae sromdk." My thanks.*

The ferryman's brittle linen-wrapped fingers caught my jaw and lifted my head. He didn't need eyes to see through me. Whatever he truly was slammed through my heart and my head. He knew I'd have consumed Hatshepsut and the entire River if he'd left me down there. I wondered if he might kill me now. He could. He *should.* Few got to swim in the River. Even fewer got away with wanting to drink the River dry from under him.

He bowed low, bringing his empty hood so close I could smell the old world on him—papyrus dust and hot reeds. "You will not return."

His words cut deep, tearing out any response I might have had. He was barring me from the River?

"Don't turn me away." I didn't care that it sounded like begging—it was.

This was my home.

He was my friend, the only constant in my life that I could rely on. The only one who'd ever listened to the boy with nowhere else to go and no one to turn to. The boy the River had given up. A soul eater among river beasts. Nameless. Pushed aside. Sneered at. Until I rose above them all and started taking the fates of others into my hands.

"Please."

"Leave and do not return until you are who you are meant to be." He lifted his head. "You, *Mokarakk Oma*, are no longer granted passage. *Your privileges have been revoked.*"

He let go, and a few moments later, I heard the boat push off the dock. By the time I looked up, the fog had swallowed my oldest friend, and I was alone.

CHAPTER 13

"You can trace physical matter, right? Use a spell to find Senenmut's skull?" I asked Shu after striding into my hotel room and finding her sitting crossed-legged on the floor, surrounded by Sesha's scrolls. She wore her hair down and tossed about her shoulders in the kind of carefree slumber-party look that, had I not been reeling from the ferryman's decree, would have disarmed me.

There were questions in her dark eyes, but after centuries cursed together, she sensed when not to push her luck, and right now I was brimming with a heady mix of shame and indignant disgust. The ferryman had barred me from my home. Not just Duat, but my actual temple home. Who in the Twelve Gates did he think he was? With Ammit gone, I was supposed to rule those halls, and he'd tossed me out like trash?

"Sure. If you let me take a sample of Senenmut's body."

I crossed the room, bit down my seething rage, and raided the minibar. A tiny bottle of local wine wouldn't be enough to dull my anger, but it was a start. I tore off the cap and turned to Shu, still watching me from her position on the floor. "Are we going to pretend you didn't take something from that tomb?"

The wine was barely more than a gulp that evaporated the second it touched the heat in my gut. I needed more. I needed all of it.

"I may have taken... a few things," she replied, tiptoeing around the enraged elephant in the room.

She'd returned to the tomb the morning I was supposed to go back there with her and found the archaeologists gone, and there was no way Shu would have walked away from an unguarded treasure trove of mummy parts without pocketing a few souvenirs. I knew my sorceress well.

"It was just a finger. Maybe one or two fingers..." She swallowed. "Some toes."

"You didn't think to suggest taking something to locate the skull?"

"If you recall, we were attacked by scorpions." She straightened slowly, deliberately, like she was in the same room as a wild animal pacing behind its bars. She was right to. "You would have gotten your panties in a twist."

"Do it."

"It's not that simple. If someone magically inclined has it —the person who set those scorpions and killed Isis's people, for example—they'll know I'm looking. We'll lose any element of surprise and walk straight into another trap."

"Isis doesn't care who killed her people and we're out of options." I raided more of the minibar and ripped the cap off something that tasted halfway between perfume and poison. "Do it," I repeated, reigning in the desire to *compel*. My compulsions never stuck to Shu anyway.

"We can still walk away."

I whirled on her and laughed. I'd never thought of Shu as naïve, but here she was, telling me we could walk away from the gods. "There's no walking away from this. The only way out is by finding the skull first and destroying it. If Isis gets it, if she tasks anyone else with finding it, she'll release whatever's caged in that hill, and all signs point to it being very, very bad for the rest of us. So do the spell and find the skull."

"It'll take a few hours. I'll need to source some items in the souk..." She trailed off, noticing how I was staring right through her.

My thoughts had wandered back to how the ferryman had barred me from the river. He'd spoken of secrets and things he couldn't say. Osiris knew what was in my mother's box, a box warded against me and made to look like a useless trinket in my hands. Isis knew *who I was*. Thoth had told me something had been taken from me, and I could feel it, an absence that couldn't be filled. Isis was using me as a pawn against her husband. Thoth had used me to kill himself. And Osiris used me to get his rocks off whenever he damn well felt like it.

I was done being used.

"Ace?"

"That's not my name." I kicked the minibar closed and set the little bottle down on the sideboard before I threw it across the room. I spread my hands, watching my fingers part. The man in me wasn't real. Had he ever been? I had power. I could wake a temple, rouse a horde of snakes, control minds with words—minds like Anubis's. I wasn't a plaything for the gods. I wasn't a man. I wasn't even sure I was a soul eater. Cat had been right. I was good at pretending, so good that even I didn't know what I was hiding. "Liar, thief..." I muttered.

"Monster..."

Isis stood in the doorway, wearing a white gown intricately embossed with golden thread. Her hair, decorated with gems, had been braided and pinned into an elaborate snake-like coil. She could have walked into ancient Waset looking no more and no less like the goddess who ruled over all.

I locked eyes with Shu, now caught between me and Isis. "Do the spell," I told her.

She nodded once, but her gaze held all the warnings. "Don't die, you son of a lizard," she grumbled before striding from the room, her head held high as she passed the goddess.

Isis didn't spare Shukra a glance and continued to gaze at me, unblinking, until long after the sorceress had left. I waited. She had all the time in the world. She could come to me. She wanted something—probably to know if I'd had any luck with Hatshepsut—but she wouldn't ask because that would give me power. So she drifted around the room, eyeing the scrolls spread across the floor, and stopped by the bed, where I'd discarded the incomplete snake-headed jackal scroll. If she recognized its contents, there was nothing to show for it on her face.

"I suppose you've never wondered why Osiris would bind your soul to such a foul creature as the demon sorceress? You did, after all, deserve the punishment, *monster*. But why Shukra?"

"Hatshepsut didn't know where the skull was," I said, hoping to steer her attention away from Shu.

"He does nothing without reason," she replied, ignoring me.

"Shukra was my enemy. I hunted her down—"

Isis regarded me side-on. Her lips lifted at the corner. "Was?"

The last thing I needed was Isis realizing I might care if something happened to Shu. "I tolerate her. What choice do I have? It doesn't matter now—"

"Choice. Yes. Choice really is an illusion, yours especially." Isis trailed her fingertips over the scroll, raking her nails along the papyrus. "How much choice do you really have with the sorceress manipulating your thoughts?"

I stayed quiet, opting to watch and read her despite every

instinct urging me ask what she meant. It was all a game. Everything. Lies and twisted truths. If I remembered that, she couldn't touch me.

"Her stinking touch is on you. It's subtle. She was careful to hide it, but she has manipulated you and perhaps continues to do so."

I laughed softly. This was ridiculous. Shukra couldn't touch me. She'd tried many times over the centuries. We'd fought, again and again, with magic and weapons, physically and mentally, but she'd always lost.

"She keeps secrets from you," Isis continued.

"I know Shukra's secrets." Even as I said it, old doubts reared their heads. Shukra had always been a formidable opponent, a demon with a soul so black I'd personally hunted it down. I should have devoured her—destroyed her—but Osiris had taken control of her fate, and mine. At first, she'd raged against the curse and against me. When that hadn't worked, she'd schemed and plotted. After centuries, we'd fallen into a mutual hatred. And now... What were we now? What if Isis was right? Could I have missed something? Could Shukra have wormed her way into my thoughts? No... No, not without my knowing. It wasn't possible.

Isis had made her way around the scrolls to me, stopping outside my reach. "Your life is misaligned. You feel it."

I should look her in the eye and show her she can't break me. But I couldn't. She'd see my doubt and know she had something to use against me. I hadn't expected this. I *was* broken. I'd been broken for a long time, but I lived like that because Isis was right. I didn't have a choice. But Shukra was Shukra. She didn't need to manipulate me. These days, she told me to my face if she wanted to fight over something.

"My poor, confused monster. How terrible it must be not to know what is real and what is a lie spun to bind you."

"What do you want from me?" I stared at the wall, careful to keep the goddess in the corner of my eye.

She sidestepped to stand in front of me, forcing my focus on her. The moment I did, I noticed all the subtle facets of her face. The way golden flecks lined her lips and darkened her skin, and how the dark, sweeping lines around her eyes deepened her gaze.

"We have a common enemy, you and I. He abuses you and makes you grovel at his feet. You despise him, perhaps as much as I do. Deny it."

My hatred for Osiris was likely the worse kept secret in Duat. Hate was too weak a word for it. What I felt for him came from a darker place. I couldn't deny it.

Isis's smooth hand settled against the roughness of my cheek. "What would you do to see his reign brought to an end? What can I offer you to help me destroy my husband?"

I caught her hand in mine to push her back, but that didn't happen. Instead, I held her hand in mine, even though it burned like hot iron.

"With my husband gone, your curse will lift. The sorceress will no longer be tied to your soul. You will be free of this human charade, free to claim your rightful place. You will be a king, a god."

With my free hand, I eased my fingers around the delicate curve of her neck and rested my thumb over the soft pulse. She let me draw her closer. "My rightful place as Devourer alongside Anubis in the weighing chambers?" I asked, searching her golden eyes for lies.

Her lips ticked. "Oh... no, my dear monster. That is not who you are."

I clamped my hand closed around her neck, choking off her air, and watched her lips part in a silent O.

Yes, this was what I was made for.

Defying gods—*breaking* gods. I yanked her close. She

brought her nails down and dug them into my cheek, dribbling blood. I knocked her hand away and turned her, pinning her against the sideboard. She could have fought me, could have struck me down— but the game continued, this time by my rules. Her pretty eyes widened. Her fingers dug into my grip.

"You will tell me who I am," I sneered, swallowing the bubbling rage before it pushed me too far. "Tell me what you know. No more secrets. I ask the questions and you answer them. You will not lie to me. Answer me, and I will help destroy Osiris alongside you."

Her smile held a vicious edge, one that excited my hungry, maddening need to claw free of Osiris's shackles. She couldn't know that the thought of being free, of not being Ace Dante, of becoming the thing I was before, was more terrifying than anything she could threaten me with—terrifying but right. I didn't want to be free. Not yet. I wasn't ready. I was still Ace Dante. What I wanted was the truth and the power to choose my fate.

I loosened my grip. Isis slammed her hand into my chest, and for a silent, blinding second, the world ended, my heart stopped, and an empty nothingness took hold of my body— until I slammed into a wall and almost went through it. The floor smacked me in the face, and the ground seemed like a fine place to rest up until my body stopped throbbing in pain.

Isis used her bare foot to kick me over. She smiled down at me, her dark skin fractured by sharp, jagged fragments of light. She kept right on smiling until I brought my knee up and kicked her leg out from under her. She fell to her knees and braced an arm against the floor, bringing her furious face too close. And then, alarmingly, she laughed. I'd expected rage, not hilarity, and before I could react, Alysdair's cold steel pressed against my neck, freezing me rigid. The goddess straddled my legs, pinning me firmly between her thighs.

"You have much to learn, monster. I think I will enjoy opening your eyes." She leaned down low, making sure I couldn't look anywhere else but at her. She could drown me in Light as she had at Karnak, but the look in her eyes was far from malice.

"Careful," I warned. "Wallow too long in the filth with the river beasts and you'll start to like it, Your Highness."

Alysdair bit into my flesh and the goddess's lips brushed mine in that tantalizing way that demanded I give chase. If I did chase that temptation, I'd fall deeper into her trap. *Maybe it would be worth it,* the reckless part of me urged.

"I will reveal all to you soon. In return, you will help me destroy Osiris." Delight shone in her brilliant golden eyes. "Agree, and you will not lose your head." She shifted her weight over my hips, drawing a hiss from me. "And other more sensitive parts."

Kill Osiris. I'd have agreed to do it for free, but the curse, and the man it made me, complicated things. Ace Dante. I wasn't ready to give that up, curse or not. *Liar, thief...* I smiled up at the Goddess of Light and lowered a hand to her thigh, testing her resistance. There was none. "I agree," I lied.

CHAPTER 14

When Shu and I were pulled aside at Luxor airport's local flight check-in, I assumed it was for a security frisk until a smartly dressed male flight attendant led us down an empty passageway and into the luxury fuselage of a private jet. His smile was a little lopsided as though he'd forgotten *how* to smile.

He offered his hand, saying, "Compliments of Isis."

That explained the glassy, dilated eyes.

Shu shot me a raised eyebrow, but neither of us was about to turn down a free flight, especially since flying private lowered the chances of security paying us attention on the return trip, with a human skull in our possession. It also conveniently kept my name off any flight lists—lists Osiris potentially had access to should he decide to track down his AWOL pet soul eater.

"How convenient," Shu remarked, dropping into a large armchair and kicking her feet up on the chair opposite her. "Isis knows the skull is in Cairo?"

Shu had worked her magic and guestimated the skull was in Cairo, probably in the Egyptian museum. We'd know more once we arrived, but it was a lead, and a good one. Her spells were rarely wrong.

I sank into an equally large reclining seat. "I told her we were investigating a lead."

Shu gave me a long, withering look, the kind that said she wasn't impressed.

"If I hadn't, she'd be here riding shotgun. Is that what you'd prefer?"

"Me? No. What about you? You're getting awfully close to the Goddess of Light for someone she calls monster."

I slipped my sunglasses on and sank low in the seat, determined to catch some sleep before we landed. "I'm handling Isis."

"Mm..."

I'd expected a quip about the handling part, but none came back. I glanced over. Shu was staring out the window at the runway rushing by beneath us.

I drifted in and out of sleep, reliving all the things I'd witnessed in the Gates, and some things I hadn't... Some burned with the memory of the Goddess of Light's lips on mine and how her brilliance had scorched in the most exquisitely painful ways.

Shu kicked me awake as the wheels screeched against the runway. We were escorted out of the airport to a waiting white Mercedes. Shu couldn't have been less impressed if Isis had arranged for two camels.

"If she knows where it is, why isn't she here?" Shu grumbled as she climbed into the air-conditioned car.

I slammed the door closed behind us, and we were whisked away from the airport. "Because she believes I'll get the skull for her like a good little man-puppet."

"Are you her man-puppet?"

I scowled at the question, disappointed it had come from Shu. "Your faith in me is inspiring," I drawled, tired of the bickering, the heat, the dust, and this godforsaken trip to Egypt.

"With Thoth's curse, you had an excuse for being a dick. But these last few days, you've been acting more like Osiris than Ace Dante."

She didn't... "I know you did not just compare me to Osiris, because if you did, I—"

"You'll what? Throw down in this car in traffic? Do it, Soul Eater. It wouldn't be the stupidest thing you've done lately."

She hadn't called me Soul Eater in a few months, maybe even years. Acehole, Ace, dumbass, sure, but I thought we'd moved on from Soul Eater and demon sorceress. I glared out the tinted window, wishing it were New York's streets we were passing through and not the dust-caked streets of Cairo. "Let's just get this over with."

I hadn't forgotten Isis's "concerns" regarding Shu's touch on me, although I'd pushed it to the back of my mind. Unfortunately, the back of my mind already harbored similar doubts, so now I had myself a full-blown conspiracy theory with Shu at its center. Was she capable of manipulating me? Yes. Could she have gotten to me without my knowing? There were ways. She was a competent sorceress—the best that I knew of. We'd spent longer as enemies than some civilizations had lasted. But I'd been watching her movements and tracking her buying activities. The type of spell she'd need to throw at me to not only manipulate me but make me forget? That required forethought and planning, and many of Mafdet's ingredients. I would have known. I would have stopped her long before she could have gotten to me.

The Egyptian Museum in Cairo was still recovering from a recent government coup, during which the museum had been raided. Through luck more than security, most of the priceless ancient artifacts had been left intact, but the world-wide attention had decimated tourism and morale. Shu and I passed through a brief security scan and entered the humid interior. If the museum had air conditioning, it wasn't working. Despite two-story high ornate arches and vast pillars, the number of exhibits rammed against the walls pulled the space in, making it feel cramped. A thin layer of dust covered the glass displays and hung like glitter in the sun-streaked air.

I fell back and let Shu wander ahead as she zeroed in on her spell's target—the skull, I hoped.

History clamored—*look and remember*—along the hallways. Artifacts from a dead world cried out, trapped behind glass. Their background magic and faint songs plucked on my nerves like a constant *drip-drip-drip* I couldn't stop and wanted nothing more than to escape. This was why I hadn't come back to Egypt. The history was too real, too dead, too close... like the things I'd seen in the Twelve Gates.

I didn't remember stopping at Tutankhamen's display, but there I was, alone and staring at the boy-pharaoh's golden treasures through a thin layer of filthy glass. A memory tugged on my thoughts—an irritating itch buried too deep for me to reach. I'd known the boy-king. I'd spent time with him, helped him end the worship of the imposter-god Atun—a jackass priest who had tried to build himself a following. He had met a timely end. Tutankhamen had returned the land to the true faith of Amun Ra and avoided war by doing so.

I drifted to another display. The dagger inside had an iron blade made from meteorite that never rusted. A gift to the boy-king from the gods, the people had said. Tutankhamen had given me its twin as thanks. But his reign, over three thousand years ago, was long before my time. I knew that. I'd always known that. So how was it possible that I remembered the many festivals when the gods had reveled freely with the people, and walking the Nile-fed wheat fields at night, and more, so much more? I remembered too much. In the Twelve Gates, I'd seen *everything*. I'd believed the visions were dreams because they couldn't be memories. They couldn't be *my* fears. Cities fallen, buildings crumbling to dust, bodies turned to ash, and the Nile red with blood.

"Ace."

Shu's hand on my shoulder shocked me back into the present.

"It's back here," she said, turning away. We headed toward a door marked *"Staff Only."* "There's no one around..."

The skull. Right. We were here to stop Isis, or whoever had attacked her people, from getting their hands on the skull and freeing the power between the valleys. I shrugged off the past and its claws. I could wrestle with those memories again later, in a bottle of vodka. Until then, I had a job to do.

We slipped unnoticed into what looked more like a storage room than a research area. Boxes had been stacked high in corners, marked with thick, sweeping Arabic writing. I smelled dried wood and baked papyrus.

"It's close. Somewhere here..." Shu pulled one of the boxes down and rummaged through bits of bone and broken pottery. I grabbed a box and started digging. Get the skull and get out of here, away from the chittering voices of the past worming their way into my thoughts.

"Ah." Shu yanked a desiccated skull free from under a collection of junk. "Finally." She beamed. "And it's ripe too. You feel that power?"

I did. The skull's harmonic hum made all the other items in the museum pale to little more than trinkets in comparison, which meant it *was* as dangerous as I'd feared. "Hand it over."

Shu's smile cracked. "We're going to destroy it, right?"

"Right. Hand it over." I held out my hand.

"Then let's do it now." She lifted the skull high, about to smash it to smithereens.

"Don't!"

Shukra's smile turned to dust and fell away. She lifted her chin. "And we're keeping it because...?"

"The archaeologists. I need it as leverage."

"Fifteen lives to keep whatever power is in that hill trapped? Seems like a decent trade to me."

"Not to me. Hand it over, Shu." I still had my hand out, waiting for her to do the right thing and give it up.

She turned the skull over in her hands, dislodging flakes of dark, paper-thin skin. They stuck to her white pants and peppered her sandals. "I think I'll hold on to it, seeing as you're all doe-eyed over Isis."

Whatever issues Shu and I had, there was no way I was letting a sorceress of her talents keep that skull. With it, she could cause a whole load of mayhem, and I did not have the patience or time to play her games.

"Shukra," I warned, "give me the skull."

"I don't think I will."

She turned on her heel and was almost at the door when I said, "Tell me right now you haven't screwed with my head and you can keep the skull."

Her shoulders straightened and the air in the room contracted, getting a whole lot colder. Seconds ticked on. Part of the museum sighed, and the walls creaked. "It's not what you think."

The bitter taste of rage burned my throat and tongue. "You *have* been in my head?" The words came out icy cold. Isis was right. Shukra had spelled me. I didn't know when or why, but she'd manipulated me. That changed *everything*.

She lowered the skull to her side and slowly turned. Her eyes looked sorry, but I couldn't trust it—or her. She'd been *inside* my head. In all these years, she'd never stooped so low.

"I knew it was a bad idea. I told you this would happen."

Betrayal cut me as deep and true as a blade. "You didn't tell me shit, Shukra. Give me the skull. I'll deal with the fallout once we're back at the hotel."

Her thumb brushed over the skull's hollow eye socket. "I can't give you this skull." The tip of her tongue swept across her lower lip. "Isis has her claws in you. It started at Karnak. You came back reeking of her then, your eyes all godlike and brimming with *her* power. You're more than in her confidence; you're in her bed. I smell her magic all over you. You're Isis's bitch."

She was wrong, but her words didn't matter anyway. They might as well have been dust, just like our fake friendship. "And you're in my fucking head!"

"I'm in your head because you asked me to, you ungrateful *boksord*! I'm so done with your drama." She whirled and burst through the door, out into the museum's cramped halls.

I marched after her, building power with every step. It was easy here, surrounded by the past. I drew on the thousands of artifacts, pulling their lonely songs into me. Too easy. More came, and the old world rushed in to my veins, stripping away Ace Dante and turning out the truth inside. But Shu felt me coming, and with the skull in hand, she had her own mystical battery backup armed and ready.

I lashed out, intent on taking her legs out from under her. Shukra spun and pulled up a shield of violent purple and black light. "You're a special kind of stupid, Ace Dante."

She snarled a short, sharp spell and lifted the skull, punching the power home.

The blow hit me and did something to my power—made it crawl back under my skin and boil me from the inside out. Glass shattered, and somewhere in all the chaos, I felt the countless little jagged daggers dig in, but pain was a symptom of being a man, and I wasn't one.

I lunged—all of me, all that I was, all that I could be, made heavy and hard by reality—and scooped up Shukra into a storm that tore into her magical reserves and ripped them apart. Her soul was there, a dank, throbbing, dark thing fringed in pulsating red. *Take it.* I could, but if I did, Osiris's curse would fling me back into the underworld and alert the god that all was not well with his soul eater.

My hesitation was all Shukra needed. Suspended in my storm, she strained against my hold, clasped her hands around the skull, and chanted twisted demon words. Whatever it was, she slapped my power back down with the same force I'd only ever felt from the gods. The skull had turned her godlike. But I was worse than any god, and it was time Shukra remembered.

I came back to myself on my knees, coughing up ash.

"Abaq hadiaan! Abaq hadiaan!" Arabic voices boomed.

Something cold and hard dug into the back of my neck. I figured it was a gun when my arms were yanked behind my back, but seeing as I was still trying to put all the pieces of my human mind back together, I didn't fight.

Shu lay on the museum floor, her dark hair plastered over her face. Out cold. Not dead, because if she were dead, the curse—

A blast of agony tore up my back, ripping me open. I heard my scream and felt my body buck and crumple. The curse. *Gods be damned, no!*

Shukra lay on her side. Security swarmed around her body, but as the curse dragged me down, pulling all of me out of one reality and into another, her body dissolved into ash and collapsed, just like the countless dead I'd devoured.

CHAPTER 15

"Well, this is... unexpected." Osiris drummed his fingers on the arm of his throne. I didn't see him do it because I was face down on the floor and having a hard time breathing, but I figured it was a throne by the elevated sound of his voice and how it echoed around a room large enough to hold his ego.

The rustle of fabric told me he'd moved. "I haven't needed to do this in a very"—closer now—"very, long time."

He rolled me over, or someone did. I couldn't bring myself to care. I blinked into the light and saw his horribly striking face peering down at me. Memories from another time and place overlaid the present, another moment when I'd lain on the floor and Osiris had leaned over me. I'd been cold then. This time, I was hollow.

He spread his hand across my chest and *pushed*, crushing me into the stone. The god's eyes blazed as he spoke the next words, turning the air syrupy on my lips. *"Mokarakk Oma, aeui ora kema em orr sremsk, orr reqak, orr kuirk."*

The curse ran steel rods down my back, arching me off the floor. It didn't stop there. As Osiris's words rolled over and over, the rods drilled deeper and deeper, sinking into my soul where they slammed home. I hit the floor, numbed and lost. Osiris brushed his hands together—just taking out the trash—and turned back to the dais. Too-bright light dazzled off his golden armor.

The curse had been broken. Had I done that?

No, not broken. He'd strengthened it. Somehow, I'd weakened it, but now it was back, locked around my soul, as strong as ever. I must have shaken some of it free when I attacked—

"Shukra?" I croaked.

"Mm..." He was far away again, words drifting. "Concerned, are you, for your condemned sorceress?"

What in the hell had happened? My body's dead weight felt as though it might burst into a thousand pieces. Fragile, so fragile. Or perhaps that was my mind. The museum, the skull, the power. Shukra had flung it at me, and I'd flung it right back. "I killed her?"

"You two had been getting along too well lately."

"Is she... alive?"

"Alive?" He paused for dramatic effect because he was an asshole. "Yes. It was a simple matter of snatching her out of time before Anubis could sense her arrival. He's been... distracted. I brought her back. I am not done with either of you."

Osiris needed her? I'd always thought she was just my punishment, nothing more. My head throbbed a deep, heated ache that threatened to eject the contents of my stomach all over this nice polished floor... wherever this was. Duat, by the piercing light and intoxicating spiced smells lacing the air. Osiris's underworld residence.

That meant Isis was close.

Oh, by the gods. If he so much as mentioned his wife, I was screwed. Did he already know? If he asked me a question and I lied, he'd know. He'd compel me to answer. My heart started beating somewhere near my throat. I willed the brittle signs of panic away. I had to stay calm and pretend this was all about Shu and me, not Isis. I could do that. I could lie to Osiris without the muddying effects of alcohol blurring my body language. I *had* to.

"What were you doing in Cairo?" He sounded casual, almost humorous.

Bile burned my throat. "A lead... Shu and me. The scrolls..." I stared at the ceiling, wishing my way through it and back to New York.

"Scrolls?"

"Scrolls... in New York. Ancient. Powerful." I'd been working on discovering where those scrolls had been coming from for months. Right now, they acted as a decent excuse for returning to a country none of us willingly went to.

My gut heaved. I rolled onto my side and swallowed the warm saliva pooling in my mouth.

His silence ate at my nerves. Any second now, he'd snap. He knew I'd accompanied Isis to Egypt. He knew his wife had asked me to help her kill him. No, not kill him. Destroy him. That was a lot worse. Killing he could survive.

"Husband..." Isis purred.

I jerked my head up and saw her sweep up the steps—all glitter and silk—to where Osiris stood watching me. She slipped her arms around his neck and pulled him down into the kind of kiss you had to stay up late to watch on TV.

I'm dead. I am so very dead. She'll tell him everything and plant the blame at my feet. He'll grind me into ashes and throw me into the Twelve Gates' winds, never to be found again.

"It seems our soul eater had an altercation with his sorceress," Osiris explained, that ringing note of humor still there. "I had to leave an exceedingly dull budget meeting to return here and resurrect the demon woman."

"Oh? I find I could not care less, dear husband," Isis

drawled in that honeyed wine voice of hers. "Come. Leave the monster on his knees or send him back to wherever the curse claimed him. His presence here is abhorrent."

"Do you not find it odd, my light?"

"I find his entire existence odd."

Osiris looked into his adoring wife's eyes. "Were you not also in Egypt?"

Isis blinked and her smile gained a wicked depth. "I was. For the same reason as he, in fact. The scrolls. There is something *familiar* about them. Don't you agree?"

Osiris pulled his gaze from his wife and staked it on me. "I wouldn't know."

Oh, but he did. The lying bastard. If I'd had room in my head for more plots and mysteries, I'd have been all over that. But while I lay bruised on the inside from the curse tearing me a new one, I barely had enough presence of mind to remember to shut the hell up.

"Send him back. I would like to know who is behind the scrolls, wouldn't you?" she asked.

A telltale muscle jumped in Osiris's jaw. "Indeed, I would." The smile he dragged onto his lips was wooden. He sank his fingers into his wife's hair and kissed her as though he owned every inch of her. She gave as good as she got, but it wasn't love driving her heat. She hid it well, so well that nobody knew or noticed how much she *hated* with her body and words.

I knew what that hate felt like, but at least I could see it coming. Osiris was blind. If I didn't hate him so much, I might have pitied the god.

Osiris peeled himself from his wife and approached me. The fear I felt was real as he gripped my shoulder. Out of all the gods, he had the power to end me for all eternity. But not today. "*I am not done with either of you.*" I clung to those words as he spoke the spell to open a doorway, and with a disorientating push and pull, he dumped my abused body back on the museum floor, surrounded by broken glass and scattered artifacts. Shukra stirred awake on the floor.

I somehow got my feet under me and stood, even as the room spun. The skull, carelessly tossed among a pile of exhibit debris, caught my eye. We'd made one hell of a mess, but with our bodies having vanished, the guards had called it quits for the night.

"Get up," I barked at Shu.

Her glare met mine and tension snapped between us. She probably didn't know I'd killed her and Osiris had brought her back. As far as she was concerned, she'd been unconscious, seconds had passed, and that was all. I didn't plan on enlightening her.

"We need to leave. Now."

She dragged herself onto her feet, eyeing the skull in my hand. She'd lost. The skull was mine. Accusations simmered in her unyielding glare. She thought I was compromised when she was the one who had compromised me.

I couldn't deal with her and Isis and the skull and whatever was in that valley all at once. First, I needed to know where the archaeologists were. Once they were safe, the skull *would* be destroyed, and I'd go back to New York to deal with the fallout of Shukra's betrayal. Osiris hadn't killed me. Everything was still salvageable. As for accidentally killing Shukra, she'd deserved it.

❧

Shukra had remained quiet during the entire flight back from Cairo, and she was quiet now as our chauffeured car bumped along the dirt roads leading away from Luxor airport. Through tinted windows, I watched the sun go down behind jagged, barren peaks, bleeding violent purple across the sky—the color as angry as the heat Shukra was radiating. She and I had a serious problem, but it would have to wait.

I clutched the gritty skull in my left hand, knuckles aching. The skull of Isis's lover and the key to whatever was hidden between the valleys as well as my leverage for getting the archaeologists back.

Shukra muttered something under her breath. It sounded distinctly like spellwords.

"Don't make me ask Isis to put you back in the locket," I warned.

She snorted gruffly and continued glaring out of the window. "I knew where I stood with Ace Dante." Her voice held a dry, sardonic edge. "You..." Without looking, she swept a hand up and down in my general direction. "I don't know who you are."

"It was a mistake to even consider trusting a soul like yours. A soul I saw during our disagreement, by the way, and it's still black as pitch. So I guess you haven't been working as hard at redemption as you'd let on. Why am I not surprised?"

She turned her cutting scowl on me. "I'd forgotten what it was like hating you. Thank you for reminding me."

"You're welcome."

"You *asked* me to take your memories."

My chuckle held its own coarse edge. There was no scenario where I'd trust Shukra enough to let her take memories. I wouldn't trust anyone with that, let alone an enemy of some five centuries. "And why would I do that?"

She twisted in her seat, angling her body and rage at me. "Something happened to you. I don't know what exactly, but you were devastated. You asked me to take a bunch of memories, so I did."

There was nothing in that sentence that convinced me. "I don't believe you."

"Believe me or not. I don't care. It doesn't change the truth."

Closing my eyes, I pinched the bridge of my nose and rubbed away a threatening headache. I'd thrown a lot of power at Shu—too much. She'd deserved it. She'd rummaged around my head and *changed* parts of me. Not even Osiris had been so bold. There are lines even the gods won't cross. Shu had scrubbed out those damn lines. How could I believe a single word that came out of her mouth?

I blinked to clear the exhaustion and dragged a hand down my face. "You're undoing this as soon as we get back to New York."

"It's not that simple. Once the memories are gone, they're gone."

That was not the correct answer. "Then you *make* it simple. Why did you really go into my head? What did you change?"

"I'm telling you, dumbass. If you'd stop being stubborn, you'd hear it. I took a few days, that's all. Days when Bast was with you."

"Bast?" What by Sekhmet did my ex-wife have to do with any of this? "I haven't seen Bast in almost a year. Not since she asked me to find..." I scratched around my memories for why the Queen of Cats had appeared in my office all those months ago and promptly left again. Whatever it was, it couldn't have been important. "*...something.* Missing women or something. I refused, and she left. I haven't seen her since."

"Nobody has seen her since. She didn't leave. I saw her with you. Right around the time your mother died and the girls were being murdered."

"What girls?"

Shu clicked her fingers. "Exactly."

This was ridiculous. "You must think I'm an idiot. I'm not listening to your lies."

"There was one girl. You took her back to your place. Scrawny thing. She looked a lot like you, only prettier—"

"Stop!" Pain stabbed at my eyes. A hangover coupled with exhaustion was kicking in. Add to that the power come down from screwing around with Isis and all I wanted to do was fall into bed and sleep it off. "Just... stop, Shukra. Even if you're telling the truth, I can't believe it. You're in my head. I can't believe anything about you."

"You're so hung up on getting answers to cryptic symbols that you aren't even asking the Bitch Goddess the right questions. Ask her about the girl. Ask her about Bast and about Osiris fucking escorts and getting them pregnant."

The things Shukra was saying sounded alien, but the passion behind them was not. It would be easier to believe her, but I didn't have the option of trusting her, not anymore. Once we were back on US soil, I'd dig up the truth, but that life among New York's sleepless streets and wailing sirens might as well have been a thousand miles and years away from this life in Egypt.

Through the window, sandstone houses had given way to rock faces and roads gouged out of cliffs. The purple sky had turned liquid red. "This isn't Luxor... Driver...?"

The chauffeur's gaze flicked to the rearview mirror. "Yessir?"

"Where are you taking us?"

"Queens Valley. Goddess of Light is waiting."

I hadn't had a second to process what he'd said before Shu lunged across her seat, fingers spread like claws. She angled for the skull, her eyes ablaze. I twisted out of her way and planted the ball of my hand between her shoulders, slamming her face first against the door. When she spluttered words that sounded as though I really wouldn't like their outcome, I clamped a hand over her mouth, leaving her nose free so she could breathe.

"Don't push me, Shu."

She hissed something behind my hand, but the spell snuffed out.

Maybe she should go back into the locket.

The car pulled up at the foot of the Valley of the Queens a few minutes later. When the chauffeur opened the back door, I shoved Shukra out ahead of me and grabbed the skull. Nobody was prying it from my hands.

Isis cocked her head at us. She was back in modern clothing, hijab framing her face, long cloak buckled against the cooling night air. I'd expected her to be surrounded by her godstruck masses again, but she was alone.

The breeze held whispers, old words and old memories. I gritted my teeth and shoved all the timeless nonsense away. Ace Dante. More than darkness. I had archaeologists to save.

She held out her hand. "The skull?"

I brushed dirt off my pants and straightened my shirt, buying time. The valleys appeared abandoned. Just Isis, me, Shu, and the driver who'd wisely returned to the car. "Where are the archaeologists?" I asked.

She narrowed her eyes. "I already told you. I do not know and do not care." She sighed and the breeze sighed with her, hissing through the dry grass. "Come, *Mokarakk Oma,* let us be done with the dead and return to the living." She turned, started up the path toward Senenmut's tomb, and called back, "The sorceress stays here."

The valley lay exposed under the encroaching night. Long shadows draped down the cliffs. Even the goddess Isis appeared small and insignificant below the al-Qurn peak pointing toward the stars.

Sucking in the dry air, I tightened my grip on the skull and started forward.

"The only power you have over her is that which she gives you," Shu said, lending the words enough weight to lift the fine hairs on my neck. "Don't forget that."

I hesitated and looked back at the sorceress with a soul as black as mine. Waning light reflected in her dark eyes, but she didn't smile. If anything, her lips turned down. I could only trust her to betray me. It had always been that way, even now when she looked at me as though she'd just said goodbye.

"For what it's worth, you won," I said. "You had me fooled. I believed you were a friend. I won't make that mistake again."

She bowed her head, acknowledging my words and their weight. "I hope your poor choices haunt you in the Twelve Gates."

"As will yours."

The air cooled the higher I climbed. Dust caked my lips and tongue, tasting coppery. I slogged a few strides behind Isis. The battle with Shu had left me wrung out and bruised to the core. I'd have preferred to be rested and strong for whatever was coming, but delaying would only make Isis suspicious. I still had the skull in my possession. I could crush it the second Isis made one wrong move. This was my game, not hers. I had control.

Isis stopped at Senenmut's entrance and peered down into the hole. "This feels right. Don't you agree—"

A rifle crack split the air a fraction of a second before pain exploded through my shoulder, jerking me clean off my feet and into the tourist information board. Wood cracked, and so did my back. Hot and fast agony washed down my chest and yanked me to my knees. I'd barely realized I'd been shot when another crack echoed in the valley. I winced, but the pain didn't come.

Isis had her hand up, curiously eyeing the spinning bullet

an inch from her palm. She closed her fingers, crushing the bullet to dust, and scattered it into the wind.

"Who dares attack me?!" she demanded, her words echoing over and over. Silence answered.

Whoever they were, they were well hidden among the shadows. Blinking my watery eyes, I scanned the rock face. Hundreds of fallen boulders provided excellent cover in the near darkness. I couldn't see anything out of place.

The skull.

It lay on the path where I'd dropped it between Isis and me.

I shuffled forward. My left arm hung numb and useless, and the pain in my chest and shoulder had turned into a throbbing heat that beat in time with my heart, but it was only pain and only my arm. If they'd aimed between my eyes—

Another shot rang out, and this time a blaze of light flooded everything, shattering my night vision but also, I suspected, stopping the bullet from finding its target: me.

"Foolish mortals!" Isis yelled. "I am timeless! Your guns are sticks against me!"

"It's not you... they're shooting at... Your Highness," I wheezed.

Isis toned down her light and blinked down at me, remembering I was behind her, bleeding out in the dirt.

Why *was* I the target? It had to be the skull.

Shadows moved among the rocks. I counted six, maybe seven, through my swimming vision. One looked familiar. Tall, slim, and young with a narrow, cocky face... I'd seen him before. Not recently and not in Egypt. Somewhere else. Somewhere far away. Another life. Another... time. Unconsciousness tugged at my vision. No, I couldn't afford to black out. I yanked myself back into the moment, denying pain its choking hold. Just pain.

I hissed as Isis grabbed my dead arm and unceremoniously pulled me upright. The goddess kept her hand spread against my shoulder, and warmth poured over muscle and bone. She avoided my eyes and watched the shadows of approaching men and women. I swayed on my feet as her healing touch stitched muscle and skin back together and tried to focus on the figures converging on the path. Gravel crunched behind me. I staggered and turned. More were coming up the valley, all dressed in black, all armed with rifles.

Isis lifted a hand and made a pushing motion, I assumed to fling them back the way she'd done many times with me. Nothing happened.

She tried again. Nothing. She released my arm and stepped forward—into a crackling barrier of light just like hers, only this one she couldn't push through or control. "What is this?" she demanded.

The skull sat an inch outside the light cage. I prodded the crackling bars. They gave, just a little, but the second I pushed harder, the barrier hardened against me. I'd never seen anything like it. Godly, definitely, which begged the question of whose godly power this was.

"By Isis," a familiar male voice began, "all that has been, that is, or shall be, no mortal man hath ever unveiled."

Isis didn't react, though I knew how the words cut her. Judging by the cocky look on the man's face, so did he. I'd seen that grin before, in Macy's. This cocky bastard was the sorcerer who'd placed a tracking spell on Shukra... That spell had brought him here. What had his master said all those days ago? Something about wanting the Dark One and my help. And then Isis had gutted him.

Cocky Steve slid his attention from the goddess to me. "Small world, isn't it, Soul Eater? My name isn't Steve, by the way. It's Avery. And had you stopped to listen to my master,

Sebek-kuh, instead of giving Isis time to find and slaughter him, you would know exactly why I tracked you halfway around the world."

"This cage cannot hold me for long," Isis announced, sounding put out but not much else. I believed her. She'd break the cage and kill everyone here with a click of her fingers. "If you want to survive this encounter, you will release me. Now."

If these people wanted to survive the next few minutes, they had a lot of explaining to do. I wasn't even sure I could save them. Nobody puts a goddess in a cage and lives. "Why *are* you here?" I asked Avery, ignoring the fuming goddess beside me.

As he crouched and scooped up the skull, his shirt cuff pulled back from his wrist, revealing a familiar hieroglyph. Priests. Oh, wonderful. Of course they were priests. But who did he worship?

"For this," he said. "For Hatshepsut. And if you want to be romantic, for love. Generations have trained for the moment the Goddess of Light returned to the Queens Valley. We knew she would return when enough time had passed and the dust had settled."

Isis bristled. "You miserable worm. Your kind should worship *me*!"

A woman circled the cage, clothes as black as her complexion and her strides confident and familiar. We'd walked the souks together. Masika came to a stop beside Avery, tucked her thumbs into her black combat pants pockets, and regarded me clinically.

"Hi," I said. It was all I could think to say, because damn, I'd been had by an archaeologist.

Masika's lips turned down. "Hey."

"When I told you the gods were real, I guess that was old news?"

She shrugged. "You clearly needed to get it off your chest."

"I saved you from her." I pointed a thumb at Isis. "That makes me one of the good guys, right?"

She winced. "We know what you are."

"At least someone does."

"You're not as clever as you think you are, Dante like the Inferno. You weren't interested in me. You wanted information about Hatshepsut."

"No, you're wrong. I wanted information about Senenmut and the skull, but—"

Isis eye rolled so hard it cut me off. "Hatshepsut wasn't even a god. Your worship of her has been a waste."

"She was a better woman than you," Avery replied with enough venom to sign his own death warrant.

A static crackle danced across Isis's clothes as the goddess contained her rising power. "Your blessed Hatshepsut helped Osiris *butcher* Senenmut." She stood still, too still, radiating a rage that reduced cities to dust. Maybe these fools couldn't sense it, but I could.

Avery stepped closer and stared down the Goddess of Light. I was looking at a dead man. "As you pointed out," he said, "she was human. She had no choice but to obey the gods. You cannot blame your mistakes on the people under your spell. But we are here to right the past." He lifted the skull and gave a single nod. "Lost to generations, we've been looking for this for a very long time. We had hoped the goddess would bring it with her to Egypt, but despite her reverent guards, we found nothing at the hotel. And here it is, brought right to us by the Soul Eater." He addressed his eager crowd. "Finally, we end this and lay this man's soul to rest."

They shared a round of cheers and backslapping with no idea of the massacre about to befall them. It would have been hilarious if it wasn't so dangerous. Avery headed toward

Senenmut's waiting tomb. He was about to return the skull to Senenmut's body, reuniting the missing piece and potentially freeing whatever power was lying in wait.

"You can't." I stepped forward and pushed against the barrier. It gave like before, but I didn't have the power to break it. Soon, I wouldn't need to. "If you return that skull, it'll free whatever Isis has trapped inside her shrine."

Avery ignored me, but Masika's glare wavered with uncertainty. She knew about the shrine.

"Don't," I whispered. "Something's down there. You told me you believe in magic. You said you feel it. Then you have to know there's another reason for all this beyond what you're trying to do."

Avery descended the ladder into the tomb, followed by three more acolytes. I had a minute to convince her to stop him, and all the while, Isis stood cool and immobile beside me, watching.

"The Soul Eater..." Masika smiled sadly. "The infamous liar." She stepped so close to the barrier that my reflection peered back at me in her pupils. I could dive in and capture her soul. The barrier couldn't stop me. We both knew it, but she turned away too soon for me to grab hold of that shining brightness inside her.

"Sebek-kuh and Avery were going to ask you for help," she explained, "knowing the Goddess of Light would soon search for Senenmut's body. Hatshepsut believed Senenmut was the goddess's weakness. Isis loved him, still loves him, and that love made her vulnerable enough to trap." She brushed valley dust off the rocks piled around us, revealing the markings of the trap Isis and I had walked straight into. "But you dismissed Sebek-kuh. Isis killed him and recruited you instead."

"Do you think I had a choice?"

"Neither did Hatshepsut when the gods ordered her to

kill the man who mattered more to her than life. Had you listened, you could have helped us."

"I don't make a habit of listening to rotting souls —*demons*."

Masika looked at Isis when she said, "Maybe you should, because there are worse things than demons."

Masika and her archaeologist priest were living on borrowed time, and Isis's growing smile proved it.

"We had a backup plan, though. Avery faked buying minor curse ingredients from your sorceress and planted the tracking spell on her as a last resort, knowing she has to stay close to you and that you would return to Egypt with Isis."

"How could you know I'd come here?"

"Because of the shrine," she replied, confusion muddying her expression. "The Dark and the Light, Night and Day..."

The Dark and the Light? "You know what's in the shrine?"

Isis slammed her hands into the cage. The world erupted in a blast of jagged white light, almost washing out my vision, but I saw Masika's body jerk and her head bend at a sharp angle, her neck broken, and then she dropped—discarded. Isis's cruel laughter filled the valley. More rifle cracks splintered the night, but they were too late. I was already dissolving into ash and shadow and streaming between the fleeing people into the tomb. Isis would kill them all in seconds. They'd sealed their fates when they trapped the goddess and killed innocents to get what they wanted. I couldn't save them *and* get the skull, and whatever I'd felt in that shrine was worse than their deaths.

I was almost at the burial chamber door when a wave of power rolled over everything, simultaneously pushing me down while lifting me higher and choking control out of me. Power. So much blinding power. The surge was alive, and real, and... *conscious*. It was all too much. I fell into being Ace

Dante, trapping myself in human skin, bone, and muscle before the *presence* could trap my soul-eater mind in madness.

In the burial chamber, I stopped. I was too late.

Blood-red light reached from inside the sarcophagus and *consumed* the priests. Avery's face withered, shrinking around bone, and his terrified eyes turned to dust in their sockets.

I watched the life get sucked out of four priests, leaving behind empty, weightless husks.

The sarcophagus lid slammed shut, and the red light vanished inside. But it wasn't over. The ground trembled. Grit rained from cracks in the tomb ceiling, and beneath the deep rumbling, all I could hear was Isis's bone-chilling laughter.

Get out of the tomb, instincts screamed at me. *Out of the valley. Run. Run far. Don't stop.*

The priests had set free something terrible and world changing. I could feel it, same as I knew the sun would rise every morning. I stumbled back through the tomb, brushing the walls and tearing away hieroglyphs beneath my fingers. *Run. Go before it sees you, finds you... and makes you see. Makes you remember...* The voice in my head sounded like mine, but the words felt off-center, like looking in a mirror. Something was wrong inside. Some deeper part of me had shifted sideways.

I was coming undone.

"Come, monster." Isis's smooth voice crooned, in my head or by my ear, I wasn't sure. The world moved, or my place in it did. "I'm taking you home," the goddess whispered, but fear had a hold of my heart. Fear that everything was about to change.

CHAPTER 16

The tomb, KV5, was everything I'd expected. Not a tomb at all, but an elaborate mazelike entrance to the vast, beating heart of power that lay beyond.

Run. Get away. You aren't ready. You don't want this.

Doubts chipped away at my sanity, but a larger influence kept me moving forward, deeper into the entranceway. The need to know the answers, the need to see the truth, drove me forward. It was here. Close.

If Shukra were here, she'd keep me level. She'd send me back. She'd stop me. But I couldn't trust her, and I didn't trust the voice in my head either. The voice sounded a lot like mine, only different—like the voice made of power and hunger, the old me who'd gorged on souls and would have continued to do so if he'd gotten away with it. The one who'd ridden out the Twelve Gates and compelled Anubis.

Stop. Don't go any closer. You're not ready.

I stumbled down a slope and shot out a hand, smudging the hieroglyphs. Paint peeled off as though it had dried only yesterday. The words, their story, beat against my hand, hot and thick.

"*Rarru...*" I whispered, needing to feel the magic reply, needing it to ground me, because all was not right inside my head. But the old magic hissed back, cutting into my thoughts.

"Kurbeddam." Forbidden. Barred.

I'd never been denied before. I yanked my hand back, stung.

These moments are not yours. None of this belongs to you. Leave. Go.

"Come..." Isis purred. She slipped a smooth, cool hand in mine. "Come and see what has been taken from you."

I pulled back, but her fingers turned to steel. "I can't..." The voices clamored, their songs turning to howls. Stay, go, run forward, run back. So many voices. So many missing pieces. So much power....

"I know, dear monster. That is why you must."

She tried to pull me forward again, but I dug in my heels. "No. What is this? What's happening to—"

Her lips were on mine, her tongue pushing in. Her mouth and her hands scorched where they touched me. *Do Not Touch —Do-not-touch-do-not-touch.* But I was, for too long and not long enough. Her light tasted like sweet poison to my oil-black soul. I didn't want Isis, I never had. I wanted her light, her power, and everything that made her godly.

She broke away and nipped at my lips, her tongue darting out. I couldn't think past her. Couldn't remember. This was wrong. Wasn't I meant to be the one in control? I'd come here to stop this, hadn't I? Something about a skull and a fight with Shukra, but all that seemed so trivial.

"The light and the dark, day and night," Isis whispered, the words hissing over her lips and into my mouth. "So clever... this lock. Impossible to break. In what world would light and darkness agree?"

I caught her face in my hands, and for a second, I fooled

myself into believing I could break free. But then I looked into her eyes, and her soul squirmed and teased and beckoned. I was already damned, so why not take what couldn't be taken? Goddess of Light. Do not touch. But I could, and I would. My grip tightened. My black heart thudded. And I locked my gaze on hers. It didn't take long. This place—KV5, the Valley of the Kings—this *me*. I was too strong here. The hungry part of me surged in through her eyes toward the soul that shone like a thousand stars. It burned and thrashed and threatened to *consume* me, but impossibly, I had it in my thrall. Even as the goddess screamed, I had her—owning her the only way I could, by devouring. I'd tried to swallow Thoth's soul and it had slapped me down, but this was different. Here, I was different.

"*Cukkomd*. Let me in." And she did. Her golden eyes burned, but she couldn't escape. I drew her soul from her center and drowned her light inside my darkness.

This shouldn't be possible.

Her light bucked and twitched, but I had her, all of her.

Monster.

I DON'T WANT TO BE THIS.

My darkness knotted inside her light, choking her.

Oh, but I do. For all the times she and her husband had forced me to my knees. For all the lives they'd had me take at their whims. For their tricks, their scheming, their control. For the girl who had eyes like mine...

More than darkness...

But I was the darkness. Wasn't that why Ammit had given me up to Osiris? To stop me? Wasn't that what everyone was afraid of?

But I'd changed. I was something else. Someone else. Someone trying to right his wrongs. I saved people. I helped them. More than darkness.

Not like this.

I cannot be this monster.

I let Isis's sweet soul slip through my fingers. I could have taken her, I still wanted to, but a human part of me clung to the tiny threads of control.

I slammed Isis against the wall. "Stay down."

I didn't see where she fell—couldn't look for fear I'd finish what I'd started. Power thrummed beneath my skin. *Hungry* power. I wasn't done here. I needed to know why. Why she'd brought me here. Why this place pushed me away and drew me in at the same time.

The voices were strangely quiet as I strode deeper down narrowing passages, closer to the presence watching, waiting, calling. Hieroglyphs glowed, lighting my path, and fizzled beneath my touch, turning to ash in my wake. Forbidden. Barred. But the old magic couldn't stop me. Nothing could.

The shrine Senenmut had constructed for Isis hadn't been *built*; it had been *hollowed* from inside the al-Qurn mountain, creating a vast cavern. Writings coated the bare rock walls, lit from within by the same invisible power that throbbed all around.

Isis's name glowed with flourishes, but this wasn't her space anymore. Despite the light, there were shadows, hungry voids that erased the writings in patches—and those shadows stalked the edges of the cavern, watching like the constant *other* presence did, but without revealing itself.

An empty limestone throne sat dead center. Unlike the walls, the stone was unmarked. It beckoned, like all thrones, but this one looked... familiar.

I crossed the floor, stirring up a layer of ash as soft as feathers. My boot dislodged the ash directly in front of the throne, revealing a mark carved into the floor. I recognized it. I'd carved it into my arm, seen it on a box warded against me, and read it on an unfinished scroll. The snake-headed jackal.

"It is all in a name," Isis croaked. Her voice traveled deep into the cavern, deeper into a larger space than the walls could account for. She came closer, chin up and shoulders back, but she couldn't hide the ashen color of her skin or the haunted look in her dull eyes. She looked at me differently now, like the second I turned my back, she'd stab me in it. She was afraid, and so she should be. It was only the small fragment of good in me that had stopped me from ripping out her soul. I wasn't sure how long that little piece of good would last.

"What is this place?" I hissed. It wasn't a shrine. Light had filled it once, but the magic here wasn't Isis's. Someone else had moved in, someone connected to me. The mark proved it.

"As blinding as daylight..." Isis whispered. She pressed a hand to her chest and stumbled forward.

"What is this hieroglyph?" I kicked the ash aside and pointed at the incriminating snake-headed jackal.

Isis's dark lashes fluttered, her eyes heavy. "Erase a name and you erase the spirit, the soul, from all eternity. From memories, from the past, present, and future. Yours was hidden in plain sight, for all to see, but no god could look closer at the monster."

"Whose name is that?!" I demanded and started back toward her. I'd yank her damn soul right out of her if she continued speaking in riddles.

Fear flashed in her golden eyes. "Yours." The goddess smiled her infuriating smile, but it vanished as she struggled to stay standing.

"You're telling me this mark is my name, my true name? Why is it here? Why did you bring me here? What else is here? You had better start talking, Isis, or I'll take more than your pride."

She lifted her hand, palm out. "Listen... Listen and I will tell you. Ammit was the only one who suspected you were not as you appeared to be. When you began consuming innocent souls, she knew only Osiris had the power to temper your hunger. But she didn't trust him with her suspicions. She came to me, told me how she had found you as a nameless boy nestled among the river beasts as though the River itself had birthed you. She found a box with you too, and your sword... Alysdair. Whenever she tried separating you from either, you fell into a rage. You frightened her. The Great Devourer was afraid of the Nameless One. She sought answers for that mark, but found none. Nothing. You didn't exist."

"Why was the name erased and by who?"

"After the sundering, chaos ensued, cities crumbled, the greatest of all civilizations fell, and millions of souls perished. You saw these things in the Journey of the Twelve Gates, but they were not fantasies. Those were your memories. You are not this man standing before me, you are not Ace Dante, and you are not the Godkiller, the liar, or the Soul Eater. And now, you are no longer the Nameless One."

For all my life, I'd wondered *who* I was. I'd thought I knew, but Isis's words, this place, this mark, they spoke of things that couldn't be. Could they?

"Say my name," I demanded.

"What if the apocalypse wasn't an event, but a man?"

I knew who she spoke of, this *monster* of hers. Worse than Seth, worse than anything inside the Twelve Gates. Only the great god Amun Ra could stand against it. Ra defeated the dark every night so the light may prevail, so that the sun would rise and life would go on. People and gods worshipped Amun Ra, and they worshipped against *Apophis*.

"Say my name..." I pushed the compulsion into the words and watched the Goddess of Light squirm under its grip. *Power. Mine.*

"Apep," she spat with a snarl. "Apophis, Lord of Chaos, a

curse, a scourge. The embodiment of evil. That is what you truly are. Your very existence offends the gods. You are the nightmare and Amun Ra's eternal enemy."

The seconds dragged on. Silence settled around us, broken only by Isis's breathless gasps. She believed I was Apophis? That's what all this had been about? Her insane fantasy of creating a villain to her heroine? "Oh, you're something... I knew time had taken its toll, Your Highness, but I didn't realize how far gone your mind was. You could have said I was Amun Ra and it would have sounded just as ridiculous."

Her eyes widened. "After everything the Gates showed you, you do not believe me?"

"I'm not Apophis. If I were, Osiris couldn't compel me. No god could touch me."

She raised a fine eyebrow. "You've hidden yourself in this... illusion of being the Nameless One, but you are not a soul eater. You are not any of the things you taught yourself to be. The truth was taken from you."

"By who?! Who could take anything from Apophis?"

"You! You are the one who stole it. What better way to hide than to hide from yourself?"

No, it wasn't possible. Sure, I was bad, but I wasn't *that* bad. "Where's the proof? This mark scratched into rock? Is that the best you've got?" But even as I said the words, the missing pieces of my past shifted into place. I'd always felt... disconnected, *wrong*, and her words had cracked open a long-hidden facet of my mind. Godkiller, Nameless One—nameless because I'd been erased. Because I'd erased myself to ensure no one could find me. But if I was Apophis, that made me a true monster—all the darkness, all the sins, all the evil in the world. Apophis embodied *wrongness* and turned it against the light, against life itself. Apophis was the End. Isis was right about that, but not about me.

I was pacing back and forth, every step another doubt, another misaligned truth falling into place. The memories that couldn't be mine, the power I wielded, the lies surrounding me.

When Isis spoke, she kept the words soft, speaking them gently so as not to break me. "Only with the combined might of Osiris, Seth, and Ra could Apophis be confined. Here, inside this shrine, locked away from time, for all eternity, or so we believed. But Apophis escaped and vanished at the same time the Usurper rose and murdered Osiris. I knew the events were connected. Apophis and Seth made formidable allies, and the timing was too convenient. I should have seen it sooner, but I had to save my husband. By the time I noticed the shrine had been breached, Apophis was gone."

Wait. What was she saying? That I was involved with Seth's attempt on Osiris's life and throne? These things had happened thousands of years ago; they were truths fallen into legends. Long ago, Osiris's brother, Seth, had murdered Osiris and tried to make it stick. It hadn't. Osiris being Osiris, he'd lorded it up over the underworld instead, and Isis had brought the bastard back, now with the new title of Lord of Rebirth. But she was implying that Seth and Apophis had orchestrated something else. A jail breakout. Apophis had used Osiris's death as a distraction to escape the shrine I currently stood in. This would make the throne behind me Apophis's and—according to Isis—mine. This was my shrine. The blank, undecorated throne was mine.

If this had anything to do with me, I'd have felt it, right? If she spoke the truth, I'd surely know it. But all I felt was... empty. Her so-called truths made me a genuine monster, and I wasn't ready to believe that. I needed time. I needed to get away from Isis and her poison. I needed to get away from Egypt.

I laughed, but it sounded strangled and wrong. "Did you

bring me all the way out here to feed me this fantasy in the hope I'd—what? Believe I'm an anti-god so I'd agree to fight Osiris for you?"

"No. I brought you here as my opposite. You are the Dark to my Light. We are the key. You and I. Dark and light, here together." She believed it. Her intense glare, the press of her lips, the solid stance all said so. "I was right, and now the end finally begins."

Isis bit her bottom lip, drawing her own divine blood from the wound, and spat it into the ash coating the floor. "Blood is paid, Lord of Red!" She lifted her voice and let it sail into the dark places. "The lock is open. The debt is paid. You are free."

There are moments that turn lives around. Moments that define each of us or kill us. As I turned my head toward the vast well of power bleeding out of the carved walls as sand, I knew Ace Dante was a joke. His little office, his bottomless bottle of Vodka, and his cursed demon counterpart. All of it was a useless exercise, like hunting for patterns in a sandstorm. The truth was far worse than I could have ever imagined.

Red desert sand pooled and swelled, forming the outline of a man I told myself I couldn't recognize, but my memory told me I knew him. Sand shaped and swirled, building up muscle and form and then hardening into armored plates. His red armor didn't shine like it would have on any other god. On this "man," it was dull like dried blood.

The man made of desert sand took up the throne, shifting comfortably to one side and resting his chin on his knuckles. His russet hair hung in multiple braids woven with gold. He looked down at his sister and then flicked his blood-red eyes to me.

"Urd kreamd." Old friend. Seth's words grated against my thoughts like sand trapped between stones. The contained

power beating against the cavern walls was his. He'd been here, trapped in the dark, for millennia, and I stood before him, broken and hollow. Whatever happened next wouldn't end well.

Gods and humans alike would drop to their knees in front of the Lord of the Desert, but I was neither, and I was only now realizing the truth of exactly who—what I was.

Seth watched me with eons-honed patience—the kind snakes possessed as they waited motionless for days before they struck and devoured their prey.

"Uir borsoem cukak su krieseum." Our bargain comes to fruition.

I'd made a bargain with Seth? Of course I had. A dangerous bubble of laughter almost pealed from my lips. I had no memory of any bargain, no memory of knowing Seth, and certainly no memory of being close enough for him to call me *friend*, but to admit how weak I was would get me killed. Seth didn't care about Osiris's curse on my soul. He'd probably see that as a reason to destroy me. To survive these next few minutes, to survive this god—the Usurper—I had to tread very, very carefully.

"I wondered if you would ever return, Dark One," Seth continued. A slow, creeping smile pulled across his red-tinged lips.

I was the Dark One? But I'd thought Shukra was... That threatening laughter clamored inside my head again. I couldn't sort through this nightmare. Not here, not now. I had to play their game and get away.

Isis dropped to a knee and bowed her head before her brother. Seth looked as though he expected me to do the same, but all I could hear was my insane laughter. I didn't feel like Apophis. What I felt like was the butt of a cosmic joke. But if there was one thing I was an expert in, it was lying to save my ass.

Seth shifted and the sands pooled around him sighed. "I resorted to sending the Rekka—"

"I know," I interrupted. "I own the Rekka. Did you doubt my word? Did you believe I wouldn't fulfill our bargain?" My heart just about kept on beating, kept blood flowing, while screams and denials tore at my thoughts.

The Desert Lord's smile cracked. "Let us not dwell on the past. Let us look to the future. You return, as the terms of our agreement bound you, and thus I am free once more. But before I ravage all those who betrayed me..." He pushed from his throne and sauntered toward Isis, parting the sands and stirring up old layers of ash so that his sand and what was my ash combined. "Sister... how wonderful it is to see you humbled."

Isis lifted her head. "Grant me your forgiveness, brother?"

"I am not a forgiving god." He thrust his hand forward, plunging it into Isis's hair, and jerked her upward, arching her against him. "You sought to destroy me!"

"You killed my husband." She bared her teeth but didn't lash out. I'd drained her power. She could have fought, but she knew better. Seth was her only weapon against Osiris. She needed him.

"And now you return, groveling at my feet for mercy. Bored, are you, sister? Are your allegiances so easily swayed?"

"It has been thousands of years. Much has changed. Osiris is weak—"

Seth laughed darkly. "I see ambition in your eyes, sister. It is not I you covet. It is my reign. Forever blinded by your light, your beauty, Osiris never understood that about you." His hand tightened. Isis hissed in through her teeth. "Osiris isn't the only weak god, I see."

By Sekhmet, I couldn't stand by and watch Seth do this to her, even if she deserved it.

"She's right," I said, already regretting the words. "Much has changed."

The second Seth's blood-red gaze turned to me and pierced deep, my misaligned soul contracted. He threw his sister down and squared up to me. Taller by at least a foot and broader too, he was built like the mountain of rock surrounding us. Unlike Osiris, who was honed for political games, Seth looked like a god who could wipe out an army with a single swing of his sword. He probably had. Maybe, somewhere in my head, there were memories of him doing exactly that. Had I stood beside him?

"The world is a very different place to what you remember," I explained.

"Change doesn't touch me." His lip curled. "I've waited long enough. Those who do not bow down will be *consumed* by the desert..." His snarl twisted into a lurid grin. "Our rightful place as rulers awaits us, Apophis. You and I have waited for this time and planned for it."

I smiled back at him, twisting it into something dark by using my slumbering power. "Until the rivers run red." But something in my answer, or my expression, must have fractured, because Seth's jubilant grin turned down and the god took a longer look at me, raking his glare from head to toe. My human appearance... just how deep did it go?

"Apophis. Dark One. But you are not him? Who have you created in you?" he asked, genuinely curious.

Well, that was that short-lived charade over with. "Yah know, that's a damn good question. Clearly, I don't do things by halves, and I did such a fine job erasing myself that I'm having a hard time dropping the lie."

"You do not remember yourself?" Seth's laughter rumbled like thunder. Somewhere beneath us, deep inside the earth, the land recoiled. "Then you do not remember our terms, and I find myself gloriously free to do as I please." He strode between Isis and me. The sands followed, draping around him like a trailing blood-red cloak.

Isis watched her brother pass and climbed to her feet. "I released you! You cannot navigate this time without me. You need me, brother!"

"I do not need to *navigate* anything. I take. I rule. And the people of this world will thank me. Those who do not will die, for I will be the God of All Things. I will be the Lord of Life." His black laughter turned maniacal.

Isis, Osiris, and Seth: Keeping insanity in the family since 3000 BC.

I shared a glance with Isis, and from the fear in her golden eyes, I figured she'd only now just realized she'd freed another monster. *Congratulations, Your Highness,* I tried to convey by narrowing my eyes. *You've heralded in the apocalypse.*

Seth spread his arms. Sand shifted, spiraled, and spilled from cracks until it washed and rolled around my feet, driven by his thirst for power. "My time has come!"

Isis reached for him. "Not like this. You must wait, be patient, move slowly—"

He struck her down with the back of his hand. A wave of sand swallowed her whole, stealing her away. When it receded, she was gone.

Seth looked at me, eyes blazing as red as the Egyptian sun, daring me to try to stop him.

I couldn't let him leave this shrine. Isis had brought me here to release him, but that didn't mean I had to let him go. I wasn't Apophis—yet. I was still Ace Dante, and that surly New Yorker son of a bitch wasn't ready to let the gods wreak havoc on this world and its people. I still had a job to do.

What the hell. It wasn't like I had anything left to live for. I shucked off the human suit and dissolved into a liquid cloud of burning ash, but Seth's sand wouldn't be swept aside as easily as mortal flesh and blood. The same terrible power I'd felt when I first entered Senenmut's tomb swelled, filling the cavern, and collapsed over me, crushing in from all sides while pulling me apart. I grappled with my writhing magic, seeking the burning radiance of his crimson soul so I could do to him what I'd done to Isis and knock him down—but he was too much, and all the secrets I didn't know the answers to had unraveled me. I couldn't stop him. I wasn't Apophis. I was just a soul eater with delusions of once being something else. Seth was a god who'd spent thousands of years plotting his freedom. He wanted *this,* and the weak thing I was couldn't stand in his way.

His power rolled me over, turning me inside out and scattering my ashes throughout the cavern. A sea of red sand poured out through the entrance, leaving me to pick up the pieces of myself. How could I make myself whole again without even understanding who or what that whole was anymore?

CHAPTER 17

Waves of sand crashed over the valley sides and flowed into the narrows as Seth's thundering power funneled toward an unsuspecting Luxor glistening against the Nile's banks. I knew the outcome; I'd seen it before. Rivers of blood, and cities crumbling.

Not now. Can't think about that now.

I poured my ash and embers down the valley after the broiling mass of sand and wind, but even if I could catch him, I couldn't stop him. He'd be in Luxor in minutes. Hundreds of thousands would die.

All those souls... so sweet, so light...

No.

More than darkness.

I could save some of them. I was still good, somewhere inside.

A blur of white car burst from the broiling sands and hurtled toward me, skidding sideways at the last second. Shukra appeared over the car roof. "Get in!"

I turned from ash to Ace and fell into the passenger seat as Shukra floored the gas pedal and worked the stick shift through sheer force of will. Wipers sloshed sand back and forth, barely clearing the windshield enough for us to see the road—if there was one. The car bounced and skidded, its engine growled, and metal groaned. Ahead, the night sky burned red.

"Are we running or fighting?" Shu asked, chasing down the storm.

"Fighting." But the lashings of red pulled away. We wouldn't make it in time.

Shu downshifted and lurched the car forward. "Good."

I couldn't stop Seth, not alone. Whatever I was, or had been, I wasn't now. I had more power than a soul eater should have, but Seth had been stuck in a tomb for thousands of years, brewing his own magical strength and insanity. I'd need the likes of Osiris if I wanted a chance of stopping this, and Isis had vanished. There had to be another way. If not, Luxor would fall, and it wouldn't end there.

"You can apologize later. I brought souvenirs." Keeping her eyes locked on the storm, Shu thumbed at the back seat.

Four canopic jars rolled around on the seat. Four ancient canopic jars that, in the hands of a capable sorceress, might buy me some time.

"You're welcome." Shu grinned.

Not all was lost. Despite our differences, I had Shu, and we had the jars. "Get to Karnak."

"We're not chasing the sandstorm that's about to eat a city?"

"No. We're waking the dead."

Her grin stretched. "You can do that?"

"Sure."

"You're a damn liar, Ace Dante." She laughed, taking too much pleasure in the insanity surrounding us.

Shu jerked the car off the dirt track and onto a smooth

road with a squeal of tires. In the distance, silent lightning cracked through the red desert storm.

KARNAK HAD BEEN CLOSED SINCE ISIS AND I HAD rearranged some of the sphinxes. The famous night-time theatrical lighting was off, the stone sitting in darkness, but I didn't need artificial light. I'd brought my own. After placing my hands on a section of wall depicting the pharaoh and gods laying the temple's foundation stones, I pushed my power and words into the old stone. *"Rarru..."*

Nothing happened.

In Luxor, sirens wailed and Seth's storm howled, but in Karnak, the silence was worse. I needed this to work. Without the old magic behind me, I didn't stand a chance against Seth. This wasn't the tiny Temple of Dendur that had spoken to me in New York's museum, and Karnak wasn't anything like the tombs that had both welcomed and repelled me. Karnak was vast, bigger than my power, bigger than Isis—had she been here—and firmly rooted in the past. But if the temple didn't wake, it might as well just be a pile of stone.

"That's it?" Shu grumbled, hovering in my peripheral vision.

"Not helping." I had to think bigger. In the entrance into the hypostyle hall, the 134 columns towered toward the night sky, some seventy feet high. I ran my hands over the stone. The hieroglyphs burned at my touch and glowed to life, but that's all the temple was prepared to give.

"I can get more juice from a fake King Tut bust," Shu unhelpfully remarked. "Let me use the jars."

"Not yet." Planting both hands on the central round column, I leaned into the stone, closed my eyes, and whispered, *"Rarru, Kormod. Woda, omd rakakbar. Rakakbar ka."* Stone buzzed beneath my hands. I kept my eyes closed and whispered the same words again, over and over, pushing my power deeper and deeper, giving it up to the old stone and its forgotten presence. *Wake. C'mon... wake and help me.* A small, distant power fluttered against mine, fragile as a dying bird in the palm of my hand. "*Cukkomd...*"

An explosion on the opposite bank of the Nile rocked the air.

"Ace..."

"Hold on... I have it."

"Have it quicker."

"Cukkomd... Listen. Remember. Know me." There was a time when the temple had sung and glowed with life and color. Its vast glory had spilled along the banks of the Nile for the whole world to see Egypt's magic and might. That world was gone, and so was its magic, but some remained, buried deep in bedrock. Like the old gods, the temple slumbered, but its fluttering heart stirred and its thrumming background resonance grew louder. It *was* waking.

I opened my eyes and stepped back. All round, light beat in waves up the columns and over the walls, filling every word, every scene. Stone groaned, and somewhere nearby, a reanimated sphinx let loose a roar.

The stone beneath my boots shuddered. The temple breathed in, soaking up latent power. Despite Karnak's stirring awake, it wouldn't be enough to stop Seth, but I wasn't done.

"The river... Bring the jars," I called back to Shu, already heading outside the temple boundaries, down to the Nile's marshy banks.

The Nile sloshed lazily against its muddy shore. Its waters were slow-moving and deceptively calm compared to the storm raging four hundred meters away on the opposite bank.

I held out my hand for Shu. She lifted her head and

looked back at me as though I were offering her a ticking bomb.

"I can't do this alone," I told her. "Whatever our differences, we have to stop him."

"What is *this* exactly?" She carefully set the canopic jars down at her feet and settled her hand in mine.

I closed my fingers around hers and walked us into the water up to our knees. I'd killed her once today already. There was a chance I might again. "I'm not Osiris. I don't have power over life or death, but there's one place I can't be denied."

Shu's grip tightened. She didn't know what I was about to do. She had to trust me.

"I'm sorry," I told her.

"What for?"

"This." I had her black soul in my grasp and her power wrapped up in mine in the time it took her to blink and see me not as Ace Dante, but as a barbed cloud of darkness. Using the great well of her power alongside my own, I spilled across the Nile water and spoke the words, *"Ovam kur ka, kur I ok uk sra oer, sra aorsr, sra resrs, omd sra dord. Ovam, omd varcuka ka srruisr."*

But instead of traveling to the realm of Duat, I brought the realm to me, opening the way through the Nile waters and calling all the wandering souls to my side. They came. How could they not? Old magic flooded the river here as it did back home. Karnak thrummed its presence the way the Halls of Judgment beckoned those on their final journey. It almost felt like home. The souls poured into this world in an eager squall of light, twitching and lunging for freedom.

"Cukkomd..."

With Shu's power joined with mine, the jars anchoring me, and Karnak at my back, I speared into all the souls and their shifting shards of light and pulled them from the river into my wrappings of power, creating my own storm. Only this one blinded, and inside, I was its black beating heart.

It didn't take long for Seth to notice. Sand billowed as high as seven-story buildings. It sloshed like liquid through the streets and over smaller dwellings, but as the god's power butted up against the riverbank, his sand diverted, bleeding left and right, *away* from the Nile. He was the Lord of the Desert. The Nile is life. It always has been and always will be. Seth's dead desert sand had no place to cross. He flung more sand at the river, again and again, his fury building with each pathetic strike. The Nile flowed on, immovable and impenetrable, stubbornly denying the god access.

I tightened my hold on the souls. They spun and twisted, rising higher and swirling harder until their combined light was as blinding as any god's.

Recognizing how he'd trapped himself across the water, Seth packed his power away inside his armored body and approached the Nile. "You summon the old world against me?!" The howling winds carried his words and the fury inside them.

He watched the souls blaze under my thrall and squirm inside the storm, fascinated and disgusted by my abhorrent power.

Typical god, distracted by shiny things.

The reanimated temple sphinx slammed into his back. Their vast paws brought the god down to his knee. Another launched from his right and another from his left. He flung them off, but more bounded in. While I had him pinned down, I called on the magic of the old world, of Karnak, of the long-dead spirit of the destroyed city Waset and the spirits of Duat. I called to all the parts that had crooned and whispered to me since I'd arrived in Egypt and to the parts that belonged in that forgotten time, that forgotten life. I threw everything I was, the souls of the dead, and everything

I could be at the desert god, drowning his desert sands in light and darkness, drowning him in the Nile's waters and my power. Drowning him in chaos and rage as I tested the truth of me.

Seth's eyes blazed red until the light, the ash and embers, the shadows and souls, tore all his unprepared chaotic power away. *I am not a forgiving god,* his voice mocked until it faded into nothing and his sands dispersed in the howling winds, carrying him out into the desert, far away from Luxor.

I dropped to my knees in the Nile's lapping waters, still clinging to the countless souls. "*Rasirm*," *Return*. It took everything I had left to force them back into the water. I spoke the words again, sealing them from this world. Barred by the ferryman, I couldn't go home, so I'd brought home to me. I wondered if that had been the ferryman's intention all along.

Karnak's power nudged at my back, or it might have been a sphinx. I couldn't find the energy to lift my head and check which.

"Kraav," I muttered to the temple—*sleep*—wishing I could do the same. The old power spilled from my grip and wound down, curling tight inside itself until all that was left was the temple's rhythmic heartbeat. Not gone, just resting. Waiting.

Seth wouldn't forget this. He'd come for me, and Osiris, and anyone who dared stand in his way, but not yet. He'd learned a lesson here—I was not what he remembered—and so had I.

I dragged my wet, cold body from the Nile and dropped into the mud beside Shukra. She stared at Luxor, the red dawn reflected in her dark eyes. Her hair hung in a knotted, sand-filled mess, and where sand had burned her face, tiny cuts wept blood. Unspoken arguments and accusations hung between us and festered in old wounds, but she'd come through when I needed her. That had to be worth something?

We'd defeated the dark for another night, and day was breaking. Seth was gone for now. The skull was back where it belonged. I'd done a good thing, hadn't I? Or had I just played a part in releasing a god worse than Osiris on the world? I'd willingly walked into that shrine, upholding the end of a bargain I didn't remember making. I was sure that didn't put me anywhere near good, and possibly on the side of bad.

The sun climbed into the sky. The Nile flowed on. Crickets started up their morning chorus.

"I try to make a difference, but I get this feeling I'm just making it worse." I spoke softly, mostly to myself, but Shu breathed in and shifted, cocking her head to the side.

"There should be a law against stupid people like you," she replied. "It's not the result of your actions, Acehole. It's the intent behind them. Even I know that."

I smiled, but that smile soon died. Were good intentions enough? Too many truths clawed and stabbed at my thoughts. Too many memories, old and new, fake and real, fought for my attention. Soon... I'd deal with them soon, but until then, I pushed it all aside and sat in silence beside Shukra, watching the sun rise and wondering if it was too late to return to being Ace Dante—or if I even wanted to, given how much of a lie the man was.

"Do you think anyone noticed"—I waved in the general direction of Luxor and the carnage the city must be waking to—"all that?"

"You mean did anyone notice when a bunch of archaeologists tried to trap a goddess because of some thousand-year-old unrequited love story? A goddess who subsequently slaughtered said archaeologists and then took her unhinged pet soul eater on a rampage through the Valley of the Kings, releasing the Usurper on the world before said goddess conveniently vanished in time to dump the blame on that dumbass soul eater? Did anyone notice the storm of souls as bright as the sun in the middle of the night? Did anyone notice that monumental fuck up?"

I scratched my chin and ran a hand through my hair, dislodging sand. "Yeah, that."

Shu snorted, climbed to her feet, scooped up the canopic jars, and stalked back toward the waiting car, skirting around one of the wayward motionless sphinxes that had frozen in her path.

"Next time we come to Egypt," she called back, "leave me in the locket."

CHAPTER 18

The weekly planner spread across my office desk brimmed with appointments. Shu's red, green, and yellow scrawls graded each appointment in urgency. Whichever way I looked at it, I'd be busy for the next few weeks. Down the hall, her phone rang. She picked it up in seconds. Another appointment probably. I'd never been so popular, and now I wished nobody knew my name so I could slink off and start fresh in another city, with another name and another life.

I swirled vodka in a glass and stared at the planner. I might as well have been staring at a foreign language for all the sense the planner made. This office, this life, why was I still here?

I set my drink down, lifted my hand, and dissolved my fingers into ash, keeping the outline of fingers and a thumb, but turning human skin into something very non-human.

How long had the past me—the thing I didn't want to believe—been in that shrine, sitting alone on that stone throne, surrounded by the dark? If Isis was right and I'd bargained with Seth to escape so he might take my place when Ra, Isis, and the rest of them cornered him, it must have been thousands of years.

Destroying or hiding those memories made a twisted kind of sense. I'd reinvented myself into something else, the Nameless One, birthed from the River with only a sword and box at my side. I'd resurrected a new me and made it so damn good that even I didn't know the truth. I couldn't argue with the efficiency of that. It had worked—until Isis figured it out and started chipping away at my apparently evil master plan.

Alysdair leaned against the wall, blade sheathed. Since Thoth had cursed the weapon to tempt me into killing him, I'd been at odds with the sword, but something else was shying me away from it. The sword knew me. It was from the old time, the old me. Was it any wonder it spoke to me every time I wielded it? It knew everything about me. And I wasn't ready for that truth.

I wasn't ready for any of this. To be Ace Dante, the dog the gods all kicked as something to do, the guy who tried to believe he was good by saving one, maybe two people a month. How many souls did I have to save to redeem the blackest of them all, mine? The Godkiller, maneuvered into the role of enemy by Isis, and the embodiment of evil that was Apophis.

Problem was, the worlds wouldn't wait for me to be ready. This was happening now. Seth was licking his wounds somewhere. He'd strike, and soon. If I didn't tell Osiris his wife and I had freed his brother, we were all screwed. If I did tell Osiris, I was screwed. Either way, my future didn't look bright. The only way I'd survive would be by embracing the truth and turning myself into the embodiment of evil. Talk about a rock and a hard place.

"What are you still doing here?" Shu strode in and scribbled something into the planner's few remaining slots for next week. "You have a ten-a.m. appointment in Newark.

Unless you've sprouted wings, you won't make it before twelve."

My ash fingers rippled. Embers fizzled along the lines crossing my palm and crumbled to dust on the planner.

Shu picked up my glass of vodka and helped herself to a sip. She turned and headed toward the door.

"The scrolls..." I said, making my fingers solid and human again.

She paused in the doorway. "They arrived yesterday. I haven't unpacked them yet—"

"Not Sesha's scrolls. The ones that have been plaguing this city by turning up in the hands of inexperienced kids..."

She leaned a hip against the doorframe and finished my drink in one gulp. "What about them?"

I'd wondered how to approach this. On the flight back from Egypt, I'd run the conversation over and over in my mind, but there was no easy way to say it. "After we got physical in the Cairo museum, Osiris intervened."

Shu shuddered. "I wondered what that slippery feeling was. The god's been screwing with me, hasn't he?"

"You died. He brought you back."

She blinked, careful to hide her reaction. "You haven't killed me in a while. I guess we were overdue." The lackadaisical words belied the thin, taut line of shock hidden beneath them.

"That's what he said." My smile was sharp and far from kind. "He also said he needed you and, among other things, mentioned some scrolls he knew absolutely nothing about."

Still, her face revealed nothing.

"He lied," I added, watching her closely.

There, a twitch, her mask cracking.

"How long have you been working for him?" I asked.

"Since the beginning." She didn't even hesitate.

"You weren't just cursed to me, were you? Does he compel you the same way he does me?"

She swallowed loud enough for me to hear and found a spot on the floor midway between the door and me to stare at. "I had planned never to tell you, but then things changed and we got busy. There just wasn't a right time."

That was the most lame-ass excuse I'd ever heard. "You had five hundred years."

"No, I haven't." She lifted her head and frowned, crinkling the skin around her eyes—eyes rimmed in purple. "Because in the beginning you were even more of an asshole than you are now. We've gotten along recently."

And that was about to change. "How far does his influence go?"

"He asks about you and I tell him. I enjoyed it, at first. Told him a bunch of lies just to see you suffer. Then, after a while, he got bored and stopped asking. I figured he'd forgotten, but then he wanted me to distribute the scrolls. Said to see that they landed in certain places with certain people—"

"They aren't just minor spells. The magic in those scrolls is so potent it's almost sentient. People have died because of those scrolls."

She shrugged. "People die falling down stairs."

I didn't want to do this, but she hadn't left me any other choice. "You got inside my head and stole my memories. Memories surrounding the last days of a missing goddess who happens to be my ex-wife. Memories that, according to you, I can't get back. And now I've learned you're compromised by Osiris—"

"Like you aren't," she scoffed.

"You're fired."

"No, I'm not."

"You really are."

"I don't accept."

"You don't need to accept. You just need to leave."

She glared at me like she could set my soul on fire at will. "Your four o'clock appointment is some hotshot movie producer who says his film set is haunted by Nefertiti's chi or shadow or some shit." She marched up to my desk and slammed my glass down. "And if you think it's that easy to get rid of me, then you haven't been paying attention these last few hundred years."

"I know I can't get rid of you," I said, calmly peering up at her, "but I can stop you from getting too close, and that's exactly what I'm doing."

"You act like you're some righteous hard-done-by schmuck that the gods all pick on, like none of this is your fault. When will you see the real problem in your life is you?"

She had no idea how right she was.

My cell chirped a message alert.

Come

Now

-Osiris.

"Shit."

What he hadn't texted was how, if he had to call, he'd compel me. I snatched up my cell, coat, and sword, shoved past Shu, and hammered down the stairs.

"Your appointments?" Shu called.

"Not your problem!"

I'd known Osiris would summon me. I'd been back on US soil less than a day and knew it was coming, but what I didn't know was if Isis was back too or how much Osiris knew about what had happened in Egypt. Did he know Seth had been roused? Did he know I'd played a major part in releasing his brother? Did he know who I was supposed to be? I was about to find out.

I should have picked up the vodka on my way out the door. I was going to need it.

I PULLED THE DUCATI UP BESIDE OSIRIS'S TESLA AND kicked the bike onto its stand. His grand neo-classical house shone under New York's thin sunlight, reminding me too much of Duat's proud columns and sharp glare.

The God of Life, Death, and Rebirth waited inside, and he could continue to wait. It was the only power I had over him—for now.

Straightening on the bike, I dug out my cell and dialed Cujo.

"It's about time you called," Cujo grumbled. "There's some new info on the break-in at Mafdet's store. Some snake skin was found—"

"And I need to hear it, but right now, I have bigger issues." I swung my leg off the bike and straightened Alysdair, snug between my shoulder blades. "Stay by the phone. If I don't call you back in three hours, pack a bag and take a vacation. Anywhere. Just get out of New York and don't tell anyone where you're going."

"All right." No arguments, no questions. He knew when to listen and when to act. "God trouble?"

I started up Osiris's driveway. Gravel crunched and birds chirped enthusiastically like this was any normal New York day.

"Some *things* happened in Egypt."

"Things like you lost your wallet, or the *we're all gonna die* kinda things?"

I kept on walking, wondering how much to tell my friend. He already knew too much. Every time I called him up, every time I brought him in on a case, it buried him deeper in my shit. Mortals standing in the way of gods fell all too easily, and Cujo was an easy target.

"Would you say I'm a good man?" I asked, marching up Osiris's steps.

The line fell quiet. He'd be wondering why I'd asked. He'd sensed the tone. It sounded like goodbye.

"The fact you're asking answers your open question, don't it?"

Maybe it did. Or maybe this Ace Dante charade of mine was good, but like a mortal's life, it wouldn't last.

"Are you about to do something stupid?" he asked. "Is Shu with you?"

"Egypt was a clusterfuck of stupid, and no. Wait by the phone." I hung up and breezed in through Osiris's front door. No guard greeted me in the vast, open foyer. I'd sucked the souls out of the last ones, and Osiris hadn't bothered replacing them, seeing as the entire house was a front. Shu had accused me of looking like Osiris, but if Isis's revelations about my identity were right, the goddess's husband and I were more alike than Shu could have imagined. I still hadn't wrapped my head around the repercussions and couldn't until I knew for certain. Being Apophis was... too much, too big, too... *wrong*. The missing box was the key, but until I found it and opened it, I'd have to answer to Osiris and pretend like everything was peachy.

"Monster..."

Isis descended the sweeping staircase, wearing a symphony of blue silken gowns that flowed from her shoulders like water. So she was alive, then. Seth hadn't killed her. Pity. This whole thing would have been a lot easier to explain to Osiris without her there to twist him around her little finger.

"Osiris summoned me," I explained, cold and direct.

"Yes." She swept across the floor and reached for my arm. A gesture too familiar for the Goddess of Light and the Soul Eater. I stepped back, making it clear where I stood. Her glower could have cut stone. "We do not have much time, and there is much to discuss," she hissed, keeping her voice low so her husband dearest wouldn't hear.

"What lies to tell him, you mean?"

"You do not understand."

"Oh, I do, and that's the problem, Your Highness. I understand all too well how you plan to set me u—"

"*Mokarakk Oma.*" Osiris didn't need to raise his voice to silence us. The barely restrained rage scratching through my name did that.

Isis and I turned toward the god. He stood on the first-floor landing, one hand resting on the banister. The sweater and black pants should have diminished his presence, but they only made the great weight of his power seem more controlled. I'd seen Osiris enraged, seen him flatten small armies and help sunder the old world beneath a sweep of his golden crook and flail to bring about a new world. The expression on his face wasn't rage. This was colder, as though all his molten rage had been poured into a mold and shaped into something harder and stronger. I got the distinct impression he was done with our bullshit.

I imagined I could hear Isis's heart racing, but figured it was more likely my own.

It didn't matter if he'd heard Isis and me arguing. He'd have to be an idiot not to suspect even the smallest of conspiracies against him. If I blurted out the truth, he'd likely kill or maim me. I didn't know what he knew, and until I did, silence was my best defense.

Osiris ran his hand along the banister and started down the stairs, one painfully slow step at a time.

Running would be the smart thing to do, but there was nowhere in this world, the underworld, or the afterlife I could hide from Osiris.

If I was Apophis, the epitome of darkness, now would be

a fantastic time to fire up that ancient mojo... Any time now...

"Husband, allow me to explain—"

Osiris lifted a hand, silencing his wife. "No, dear wife, allow *me* to explain." His penetrating dark-eyed gaze slid from Isis to me, noting how the goddess stood too close to his pet soul eater. Isis took a step away, cementing her guilt. It would have been hilarious had I not been about to get my ass handed to me.

"You"—he nodded at me—"followed Isis to Egypt. *You* followed her to the Valley of the Kings where she hoped to find the lost body of her lover." Isis winced, but her husband only had eyes for me. "There, *you* stumbled upon Seth's prison and *you* freed the Usurper as vengeance against my control over you."

When he put it like that, of course I looked like the guilty party, exactly as Shukra had suggested, exactly as Isis had whispered in his ear, and exactly as I'd known all along how this would play out.

It was time to find my voice. "Why would I follow Isis to Egypt?"

"You are not the first to love the Goddess of Light."

I almost laughed in his face. *Love* Isis?! He was the only one alive and crazy enough to fall into that trap. But to deny it would insult them both. Still, insulting Osiris had to be better than getting strung up, drawn and quartered, and left out in the sun to bake, like the last poor bastard who'd fallen in love with Isis.

"You know the problem with gods?" I growled out. "You all believe your own divine PR campaigns."

Isis shifted, quietly moving behind her husband in a submissive position. A good place to be, because I was done holding my tongue and dancing around truths and prophecies and lies, so many lies.

"I don't love Isis. I don't even like her. I don't hate her quite as much as I hate you, but it's a close call. She's a grade-A sociopath, and so are you. So are the rest of the gods awake and breathing today. Driven insane by time and power, you're so consumed by your own divinity that you can't see it for what it truly is: a noose around your necks. Your world is dead. Your time is dead. Get over yourselves. You could do a lot of good in the new world, but you can't see past your own egos to try. That makes you a bunch of hypocritical, inbred assholes."

They'd both fallen still and silent, but I had plenty to say to fill that silence.

"Isis believes she can use my desire for her against me, and she did, but let's not mistake desire for love, Osiris. You're not an idiot. It's not even your wife I want, it's her power. So sure, when Isis asked me to go to Egypt and threatened to tell you how I wanted to get her in the sack, I figured a trip back home was the lesser of two evils. I was wrong, but then I'm wrong about a lot of things—like who I really am..."

A nerve twitched under Osiris's eye. Maybe he had something he wanted to say, but I wasn't finished.

I pointed a finger at the suspiciously quiet Isis. "I went to Egypt to retrieve a skull for her on the premise that she didn't want you knowing how she was chasing after a lost love. I didn't want to go back. I never have. I've avoided that place for hundreds of years, thinking it was my choice not to go back. But now I know why I've never wanted to go back."

"He's a fool and a liar," Isis sneered.

"No! What I am is tired of shoveling your lies, Your Highness."

Osiris, now as still as the many statues of himself, watched, waiting for me to tighten that noose around my neck.

"Your wife killed Ammit," I said. "Your wife forced me to

go back to Egypt, and, in all honesty, I don't think she cares about an ancient love, because as she admitted, time has sapped her ability to care about anything but herself. She didn't want to find a desiccated corpse; she wanted the key to Seth's tomb. The key was me and her working together. All that light, and she's as rotten in her core as I am. Osiris, your wife wants you gone. She's tired of living in your shadow, but she can't come at you head-on, so she used me, Thoth, and probably countless others over the years to undermine your reign. And now she's released Seth, the only god who can knock you off the top spot. So sure, pin all the blame on me if you want. Let her distract you. Really, at this point, I'm already screwed. Just know that as much as I hate you, when you fall, and you will, it wasn't by my design. Look no further than your bed to find your enemy, or continue to be blinded by her light. What do I care? I'm just the Nameless One..." I hadn't realized how close I'd gotten to Osiris, but as I squared up to the god and looked him in the eye, I should have been afraid, but I wasn't. I wasn't the Ace Dante he controlled. Not anymore. "I'm just some wayward orphan son Ammit found in the mud, right?" He didn't blink or turn away, and as my hunger rose, soul-eater urges took hold. I whispered, "Do you keep me controlled because you know I'm a lie?"

"Husband, silence him."

But Osiris was listening and those dark eyes of his held my unblinking glare, waiting for me to crumble. But I wouldn't because the truth was out and holding me up.

"Ask yourself," I said more quietly and so close to the god that my words were almost intimate, "did I release Seth or did your devoted wife?" For the first time in five hundred years, Osiris looked back at me, not as a tool, but as an equal. My words traveled soul deep where he couldn't deny them.

His hand locked around my throat, crushing tight. I

brought my arm up to break his hold, but his grip was stone. *Alysdair*.... I reached behind...

"You are right," Osiris snarled. "Thank you, *Mokarakk Oma*, for opening my eyes to the truth."

My fingertips grazed Alysdair's hilt, but I couldn't grab hold of it.

His fingers tightened, threatening to snap my neck. "You are both traitors." Osiris flung his free hand out, blasting heat and light toward Isis, but I couldn't turn to see the outcome. I heard her piercing scream though, and then silence.

Osiris's grin was a twisted thing, made of poison and vengeance, jealousy and insanity. He lifted me off my feet. "So many secrets. Let me reveal one to you. My eternal love for my wife is matched only by my wrath. When I learned of my wife's affair, I ensured Senenmut's soul was sealed inside his sarcophagus. His mortal body crumbled, but his soul burned on for centuries, trapped. How will your soul fare trapped in stone for eternity?"

In a blink, we were gone from the entrance hall and inside a small dark room that reminded me of the Cairo museum. Intense spotlights illuminated an unmarked stone sarcophagus. A modern-day tomb, likely hidden beneath his house or somewhere inside its walls, and I was about to become its resident.

I thought of sand and shadow and all things—

"*San*," Osiris growled, stopping my change dead in its tracks. "*Cukkomd*." The compulsion sank its fishhooks in, driving them so deep that when he released his grip, I couldn't move. Just like all the times he'd frozen me inside my skin, I couldn't reach Alysdair against my back or lift a hand to stop what was coming next.

Osiris shoved the stone sarcophagus lid aside, the sound rumbling like thunder. "Place the sword inside."

I pulled Alysdair free and laid the sword gently inside the sarcophagus.

"Climb inside."

As the words wormed into the part of my mind susceptible to his commands, I wished I were Apophis, or anything or anyone else, so I wouldn't walk into this forced slumber—because that's what this was. My mind wouldn't survive. I'd have to sleep to survive; otherwise, trapped inside the stone, I'd go insane.

My trembling hands gripped the six-inch-thick stone rim. The rage boiling my insides and the fear icing up my heart did nothing to stop the inevitable. If I was a monster, then now was the time for the truth to come out. If I was Apophis, why couldn't I save myself? Why was I climbing into my own coffin?

I fought the compulsion and pushed back against Osiris's hold—shoved with everything I had, every rage-filled Ace Dante part of me. Cracks appeared, and needle by needle, I unpicked his mental grip. But not fast enough.

"This is a mercy," Osiris said.

I sat inside the sarcophagus and stretched out my legs like the lamb to the slaughter.

"I told you the truth, and this is how you repay me?" The words trembled off my tongue.

"Lay back."

I did.

Osiris leaned over and braced an arm against the opposite side of the sarcophagus, bringing him so agonizingly close, yet so far out of my reach. I'd have sold my soul and the souls of a dozen innocents to punch that smug face. My hand twitched, but it wasn't enough. Given time, I might be able to break free of his compulsion—that alone was a testament to either his waning power or mine growing. But I'd run out of time.

"The truth is," he sighed, "I must do this. I am the custodian of this world. I've been preparing for my brother's return since the moment we imprisoned him. I cannot allow him to ally with you. This world, with all its technology and electronic infrastructure, is more fragile than the last world Seth helped destroy in the sundering. My brother has the ability to crush this world, and you would stand beside him. I know you. I've always known you."

"You *knew* me, Osiris. But today, I am not Apophis."

"You will be."

"Then kill me. Better that than..." *Being buried alive in eternal darkness.*

His smile was a sorry thing. I wanted to rip it off his lips.

Fear. I was familiar with it, but not this brittle terror. The sarcophagus lid would slide closed, plunging me into the dark, and I couldn't stop it. I'd been helpless before, like when he'd commanded me to kill or dropped me to my knees with just a word, but this...

"Do this and there's no going back. Trap me in here and when I get out it won't be Seth hunting you down. If I am Apophis, then you know what I'm capable of."

He hesitated, and so he should. As Apophis, I could destroy him. But the hesitation faded behind a flicker of righteousness I hadn't known he possessed. "Some of the past should be left buried, lest we repeat the same mistakes." The lid shifted, stone grinding on stone. Already the light was fading. "You are a good man, condemned by your past, shackled by the lies of your future. But that part of you is a fabrication, and it is breaking down. I must do this, and you already know it. If you could stop the apocalypse by condemning one man, you would."

Stone rumbled and shook. Grit crumbled. The lid closed, and the light shrank until only a sliver was left, and then that too vanished. All around me was nothing but darkness—a darkness with a weight to it that tasted like blood and felt like ashes on my lips. A darkness of my making. I raged and spat curses and vowed to destroy Osiris, but the darkness surrounding me came to life, and too soon, it drowned me in its poison.

CHAPTER 19

It didn't take Shukra's betrayal, or Isis's manipulation, or Seth's attack for me to believe. Osiris's having me crawl into what would be centuries of torment broke the lies open, revealing the truth inside.

As I dwelled in my own poisonous darkness, hours, days, weeks passed. Time became nothing. I saw cities crumble, deserts rise up and swallow entire towns, and I started to believe.

"I am Apophis." The words drifted, rough but insubstantial like ash.

I curled my hand around Alysdair's grip, and the sword came alive. Its ancient song hummed, and its magic poured up my arm. The sword knew the truth. It always had. I just hadn't listened.

Apophis. End of All Things.

"I am Apophis." Harder. Firmer. Real.

Time flowed. The familiar darkness was all I had to cling to. Osiris's compulsion fell away like rusted cage bars. I pressed my left hand to the inside of the sarcophagus lid and pushed.

"I *am* Apophis." Truth.

The lid creaked and shifted. Grit rained over my clothes. Dark waves of my true, unhindered power rolled over me. And then a thin line of light opened, guiding me toward freedom.

For too long, I'd lain in the dark, hidden, unseen, nameless.

Nameless no more, I pushed the lid from the sarcophagus. It toppled and hit the floor, cracking on impact. I climbed from inside my coffin, the sword ablaze and as hungry as I was. Not for life, or good, or love, or all those Ace Dante things, but hungry for vengeance. Hungry like only a god knew hunger.

"I am Apophis, nameless no more."

As I headed for the door, a distant voice whispered across my ragged, ancient soul, *More than darkness.*

Ace's adventure continues in Serpent's Game! Read on for the first chapter!

Click here to buy Serpent's Game today.

SERPENT'S GAME, SOUL EATER #5 - EXCERPT

New York.

Eight point four million souls.

From my viewpoint crouched on the rooftop, they flickered and glittered in my vision like countless city lights scattered across the cityscape. If the rumors about me were true, I had the potential to reach out and capture every single immortal soul in my hands and swallow them down. It wasn't like I hadn't tried before. I'd failed, but I hadn't known who —what I was then.

Apophis. Evil incarnate. It's one thing to hear you're the biggest bad there ever was, and another to believe it. And I did believe. I didn't have those memories or that power, but I believed they were locked away inside me. A gift to myself. A way to hide in the modern world. And it had worked —until Isis.

I wasn't fully Apophis yet, but the truth was inside me, slumbering like the old gods. That made me dangerous.

Movement down on the street caught my eye. A man

moved through the late evening crowd, collar up, chin tucked against his chest, his pace brisk.

I straightened and walked along the roof, keeping him in my sights.

He jogged across a side street, weaving through stationary traffic. The glance over his shoulder sealed it. I got a look at his face, tight with concern and guilt, but in his eyes, a glimmer of truth exposed him. Joseph Aaron, fresh out of prison where he'd learned a few new magic tricks, like how to siphon magic and hoard it. Most witches worked in covens, but not him. Joe was a loner and up to trouble.

I tapped my earpiece. "I've got him."

"Where's he heading?" Cujo's small, disembodied voice came back.

"East Sixty-Eighth. Looks like home."

As Joe turned left below, I followed my rooftop path and took a running leap to the next building, keeping Joe's hasty getaway on my right. He had no idea a monster was watching him. I almost felt sorry for what was about to happen. Almost. He'd stolen magic and used it to manipulate people around him. If he wasn't careful, he'd have worse things than me coming after him—things that would use his stolen, compromised magic against him and against innocent people who didn't know any better.

Joe stopped beneath a spindly tree and broken streetlight, looked around him to check he was alone, and dug into his pocket, probably for a cellphone. He should have been heading straight back to his apartment. Something had spooked him. Likely me.

"Ace?" Cujo's grumble sounded in my ear. "Remember what we talked about?"

"I'm good." I stepped up to the edge of the roof.

"We both know that's a lie."

I chuckled at the sour note in my friend's voice and

stepped off the edge. Five stories sailed by. I landed in a crouch, feeling the impact through my bones but riding it out. Joe spun and watched me straighten, watched me lift my eyes to his. Alysdair hummed melodically against my back, ever hungry. My duster coat—the second in recent months—had gained a few new battle scars. I knew the picture I painted, as did most who followed the urban legend of the Nameless One. He recognized who I was, but he couldn't know *what* I was.

He flung his cell at me—the only thing he had in his hand. I leaned to the side, and it flew right past. It shattered against the wall behind me.

"I hope that wasn't the latest model?" I asked. He had more magic than most people in this city, and he'd thrown his phone at me? I'd be lying if I said I wasn't disappointed. I stepped forward.

Joe cowered back. "Wait." His bottom lip quivered. "I don't have any cash. Don't hurt me."

His clothes were tatty, and his chin was a mass of whiskers. Everything about him screamed that life could have been kinder, but the truth was in his eyes… and his soul, which slithered and knotted inside him like a bucket full of eels. "Didn't anyone ever tell you you can't lie to a soul eater?"

He knew then that his act was pointless, and from one blink to the next, his vagrant act peeled apart. His glamor dissipated in a fine mist, revealing the sharply dressed, keen-eyed individual beneath. His fear had vanished, replaced by an aura of smugness and a sharp smile on an even sharper face. He lifted his right hand.

"Catch me if you can."

With a click of his fingers, he vanished. Gone. Or so it would seem. But I was aware of his MO. I'd been watching him since Cujo had tipped me off about the jewel and fine arts thief that apparently disappeared in front of security cameras.

He hadn't chosen the spot beneath the broken streetlight by accident.

At my feet, where the tree branches cast skeleton shadows, those shadows rippled like a sheet lifting around something hidden beneath. I watched him sneak off inside those shadows. Hiding in shadows wasn't an easy trick to pull off.

"The thing about borrowed magic is," I said, following the shadows as they stretched out and bled into each other, "it'll never be as strong as soul-born magic. The second you've severed it from its source, it's compromised."

I trailed after the shadow and watched it crawl up a wall and around a corner into a quiet, leafy residential street. The first streetlight popped and died, and the shadows continued to *move*.

"So when someone like me comes along," I continued, striding alongside the shadow, "it's almost too easy to take it back."

I plunged my hand into the shadow, appearing to bury my arm up to the elbow in the wall. Joe's slithering presence recoiled, but I was done playing games with this fool. I yanked him free from his hidey-hole and slammed him against the wall. Something cracked. Pain flitted across his eyes. He wasn't smiling now.

"Didn't it ever occur to you that something might come looking for that magic you stole?" I leaned in, letting him get a good look at my eyes. Whatever he saw there widened his gaze until tears swam in his vision. My grip tightened on his neck, choking him. "There are worse things out there. Things you could only imagine in nightmares." His soul recoiled as I rooted around inside the man's eternal life force because he needed to understand. "This isn't a game. This magic isn't your ticket to whatever you think you deserve. It's your death looking you in the eye."

"Ace..." Cujo queried from so very far away.

I ignored him as easily as ignoring a fly.

"You have no idea about the creatures that would gladly sup on your soul as though it were nothing but a delicious treat before the main feast."

Joe's eyelids fluttered and his pupils widened, allowing me to delve deeper. He had no defense, no means to stop me. His hoard of borrowed magic and its tricks weren't enough. I tilted my head as I studied the things I found inside this mortal man. Dreams dashed. Lives ended by his hand. Not just a jewel and magic thief, but a coldhearted killer too.

"We're the same, you and I." My voice had taken on an edge and an accent that curled and flicked, laden with the old world and the old language, with sand and smoke. The edges burned.

This killer's soul was mine.

Something bright white and barbed snapped down my left arm, through my shoulder, and struck somewhere in my chest. I recognized it as pain, but I didn't feel it as such.

"Ace, you sonofabitch, don't make me wheel my ass down there!"

Cujo's voice joined that detached pain and pulled me back from the brink, back into my skin. Shock did the rest. I dropped Joe and forced myself back three steps, almost stumbling into the street. The magic thief spluttered and wheezed on his knees, drawing in breaths like they were his last.

I lifted my left hand. The sleeve fell, revealing the slave cuff beneath. It glinted under the pale light. A reminder. A precaution. It had worked.

"Cops inbound," Cujo barked. "Get your ass out of there. Now!"

I locked glares with the wan-faced Joe and narrowed my

eyes. "Your trinkets and jewels were either destroyed or returned to their original owners. Mark my words, thief. I know you, and I will find you. I suggest you try to—"

The gun was unexpected. So was the shot. But there it was, in his hand, and there I was, turning into the kind of hungry shadows that made his look like mist. My smoke and ash were made of the things he called nightmares. I didn't speak the words, didn't judge him. I just swallowed his soul in one satisfying embrace.

"*Daquir*," I whispered, twisting now-human lips around the word and turning Joe's remains to dust, scattering the thief and killer into New York's diesel-tainted wind.

By the time the cops rounded the corner, sirens wailing, I was a block away, collar up. I hid the sword at my back and strode into the late evening flow of people with a sated smile on my lips.

A NOTE FROM PIPPA ON RESEARCH

KV5 is a real tomb in the Valley of the Kings. Excavations have been underway for years. It is the largest tomb in the valley and one I've always been fascinated by. As Ace mentions, KV5 does not have a typical tomb layout, so there is speculation as to exactly what the 'tomb' was for, if not for a sarcophagus. Archaeologists continue to make discoveries there today.

Likewise, Senenmut is real, as is the mystery surrounding his death. An important man in his time, he was Hatshepsut's chief advisor and possible lover. But his body/tomb has never been discovered. It could be that he was murdered by Hatshepsut's nephew and rightful pharaoh, or that we simply haven't found the right tomb... yet.

Egypt has not yet given up all of her secrets. There are still many mysteries to uncover beneath the sands. Perhaps, even some gods?

I adored adding some of these facts into Ace's adventure in Egypt. I hope you enjoyed reading them.

ALSO BY PIPPA DACOSTA

The Veil Series

Wings of Hope - The Veil Series Prequel Novella

Beyond The Veil (#1)

Devil May Care (#2)

Darkest Before Dawn (#3)

Drowning In The Dark (#4)

Ties That Bind (#5)

Get your free e-copy of 'Wings Of Hope' by signing up to Pippa's mailing list, here.

Chaos Rises

Chaos Rises (#1)

Chaos Unleashed (#2)

Soul Eater

Hidden Blade (#1)

Witches' Bane (#2)

See No Evil (#3)

Scorpion Trap (#4)

Serpent's Game (#5)

Edge of Forever (#6)

Science-Fiction

Girl From Above #1: Betrayal

Girl From Above #2: Escape

Girl From Above #3: Trapped

Girl From Above #4: Trust

New Adult Urban Fantasy

City Of Fae, London Fae #1

City of Shadows, London Fae #2

ABOUT THE AUTHOR

Born in Tonbridge, Kent in 1979, Pippa's family moved to the South West of England where she grew up among the dramatic moorland and sweeping coastlands of Devon & Cornwall. With a family history brimming with intrigue, complete with Gypsy angst on one side and Jewish survivors on the other, she draws from a patchwork of ancestry and uses it as the inspiration for her writing. Happily married and the mother of two little girls, she resides on the Devon & Cornwall border.

Sign up to her mailing list at www.pippadacosta.com

www.pippadacosta.com
pippa@pippadacosta.com

Made in the USA
Monee, IL
19 July 2020